GOD AIN'T SPELLED GOVERNMENT

BY

KIM ROBINSON

Publisher's Note

This is a work of fiction. All events in this story are solely the product of the author's imagination. Any similarities between any characters and or situations in this book to any individuals, living or dead, or actual places and situations are purely coincidental.

DEDICATION

I always said that I wanted a book in every genre, and this is science fiction. Of course, there is some romance and comedy included. I started writing this book in 1997. I set it aside and forgot about it.

When the pandemic came about, I stumbled over the file, and to my surprise, a lot of the content had come to fruition. The fiction that I thought was fantasy is now reality.

I want to thank my friends and dedicate this book to my uncle, Johnathan Broussard who encouraged me to finish this book, and to those who have given me their input, The Writers Block, Black Pearls Keepin' It Real Book Club and Von Howard.

CHAPTER 1
JUNE 1997

The government's attempt to explain the rash of UFO sightings as hallucinations and air force testing was successful. Had the truth been known it would have resulted in global panic. Government officials from all corners of the world were meeting in Roswell, New Mexico. They were meeting with aliens. These were not the kind that came across the Mexican border or were smuggled into the country from China or Russia, these aliens were from outer space.

The aliens hailed from an uncharted planet whose natural resources had been exhausted. Power struggles led to the deployment of nuclear weapons of mass destruction that resulted in elevated levels of radiation rendering the planet uninhabitable.

Contaminated food sources and incurable diseases ran rampant leaving a skeletal population. Mutant infants survived no more than six months before perishing. They organized and put their efforts into building spacecraft to enable them to leave the planet. Everyone underwent a physical examination to ensure they were free of disease before obtaining permission to board.

Once the aliens on the fleeing ships attained a safe distance, they mercifully exterminated the remaining populace. The survivors spent light years exploring planets in hopes of finding a place where they could exist. Their physical traits were incapable of adapting to certain atmospheres and there was not enough time to erect environmentally friendly structures.

Earth's atmosphere was their best bet to avoid extinction.

Human officials listened as aliens explained that they had come to Earth more than two hundred years ago. With the help of medicine their lungs were able to adapt and process air, "The last few decades Earth's atmosphere has become so polluted that it has become necessary for us to inject ourselves weekly, rather than monthly, with an enzyme that enables our bodies to process and eliminate the contaminants that are causing the fatal physical maladies that your race is succumbing to."

Another alien stood, "We could have easily taken control of your planet at any time. When we sent our first teams here to investigate, this was our intention, however, we have no desire to repeat the mistakes of our ancestors. Not to mention we have grown quite fond of humanity. As we studied your habits, we discovered you are not hugely different from our race. The only advantage that we have is the fact that we evolved twenty millennia before you."

A woman stood, "We do so enjoy the creature comforts that you have developed. Our sustenance consisted of bland wafers processed from our dead. We soon discovered that this aided and accelerated the spread of disease and it was not as enjoyable as your fare, my favorites being the Italian and Mexican cuisine."

"Also, your methods of reproduction are much more enjoyable

than our incubation chambers. We cannot procreate successfully with each other as we have delightfully been able to do with you humans," the assistant to the Czar said.

The officials all turned and looked at him, "What do you mean, we? The Czar asked, moving his chair away from his assistant who was changing right before his eyes.

Their physical appearance was abhorrent to the humans. Fear vibrated through their hearts as the comprehension of these words brought them to the realization that they had been spending every day of their lives working and entertaining aliens.

"This is an atrocity. I for one do not plan to allow you to take over our world," The prime minister of Russia said as he stood to leave. Four comments were muttered that supported his views. When he got to the door, he found that he could not open it.

"Just how do you presume to stop us when you cannot even leave this room unless we allow it? We are going to live on this planet with or without you, it is your decision," The First Lady, Rosalyn said.

The room fell quiet as the Russian reluctantly returned to his seat. The President of the United States was aghast as he watched his wife of thirty-six years morph into alien form. He never had a clue, "We have kids together. What about our children? Are they your species or human?"

The look on his face told her that her natural appearance repulsed him. She would have to use her mental capabilities to change his views. It would not be hard; they had been implementing their thoughts and decisions into Earthling's undeveloped minds since they arrived.

She morphed back to human form, took his hand in her own, and laid the other on his face affectionately, "Unfortunately your genetics are stronger. Our children are human."

She neglected to tell him that by the time they turned forty alien traits would start to surface.

Several politicians rose and proved that they were aliens. Each one held key positions making them the primary decision-makers of human governments. The White House, Parliament, the Vatican, The Kremlin, every country had at least four aliens in power.

The aliens morphed back into human form. The President of Cuba was amused by the childlike tantrums the human rulers displayed. As he walked around the room, he said, "We shared our technology with you, our simpler creations such as microwaves, lasers, and satellites. Instead of utilizing these things for good, your scientists experimented, changed, and distorted these inventions into weaponry for the senseless wars that your countries wage on one another."

The First Lady stood, "Medicines were availed to you that could have cured any medical malady including the Ebola virus, Aides, cancer, flu, pneumonia, heart attacks, lung, and kidney disease. Instead of dispensing to the sick and dying, your pharmaceutical and insurance companies greedily hoarded them for their agendas instead of curing the poor and middle classes, only the richest of the rich received cures."

The Pope stood, "If you could all join hands and close your eyes, we will show you why you need our knowledge to save the human race and this planet."

They hesitantly complied. It was as if they were watching a movie. They saw Black and Asian slaves taken from their villages and placed on boats where many died of starvation and disease and were thrown into the sea. Human traffic victims were sent to their deaths because they attempted to fight for freedom.

Once at their destination, they watched people being sold on auction blocks and forced to work under unspeakable conditions. Flashes of gang fights and drive-bys, the holocaust showed Jews being taken from their homes to live in camps where they were exterminated much like bugs. Biological warfare flashed through their minds.

Visions of women being raped down through generations resulting in retarded, handicapped children. Family members commit incestuous acts on their own offspring and siblings, making their futures bleak, dismal, trauma-filled existences.

Prisons overflowed with young men who would never be allowed to live up to their full potential for crimes that were minor compared to the government's atrocities.

They cringed at the site of bombs dismembering and beheading men who were too young to die in senseless wars. Abraham Lincoln, The Kennedys, Martin Luther King and Malcolm X fell to the ground as they were assassinated. They shrank in their chairs as bombs decimated ships in Hawaii, Japan, and Europe.

They viewed train cars left on the tracks in ghettos, knowing full well that the abandoned cars would be investigated by people looking for something to supplement their meager incomes, or the homeless looked for someplace to sleep out of the rain. The guns and automatic weapons they found resulted in decades of genocide.

Livestock injected with steroids grew abnormally large, the same steroids remained in the food after it was prepared for human consumption, causing an influx of obesity and heart disease. Food stamps were made available for the asking within the communities of government-aided housing and Section 8, keeping them contained in desired areas.

The government flooded the ghettos and barrios with alcohol and drugs which further crippled the minority races. The plan backfired as drugs leaked into their sheltered communities through their children, who now sat in expensive rehabilitation centers getting their lives back, while financial assistance for Medicaid was cut to the bone.

"Wars threatening nation against nation wiped out all plant life. The nuclear, biological, and chemical weapons did not play favorites. Even the person who detonates the bomb will be affected unless there is a place to wait out the next two years while the Earth regenerates and cleanses itself as our planet has been doing for the last fifty years," The Prince of Iraq said.

"As much as I enjoy some of the creature comforts that you humans afford us, do not make the mistake of thinking that our existence will be secondary to sentiment, we can always clone you. This is going to happen with or without your compliance," the Czars assistant said.

Rosalyn stood and said, "We suggest that things go on as they have been for now, we will give you one week to deliberate. We propose the construction of a shelter that would house approximately two hundred thousand disease-free humans who have occupations that will contribute to the reconstruction of Earth."

The aliens took their leave while the humans sat in silence trying to process this information.

Knowing that they had no choice when they met again the next day, they were all in agreement and began working out the details - rather than die, they would cohabitate.

CHAPTER 2
GORDON

G ordon Wallace joined the Navy right out of college, where he furthered his education. Upon his discharge with honors, he enrolled in a D. C. college to get his degree in psycho-human behavioral studies.

The government was grooming him for a position that he would be stepping into with the Department of Defense upon his graduation this year. He was always an overachiever, focusing on his education and career.

His parents had left him on the steps of a New York orphanage when he was a few days old, no note, no name. If he could find them, he wouldn't want to. What could he possibly have to say to them?

He bounced from one group home to another. He was nothing more than a monthly paycheck to the foster parents who took him in. Now and again, when he still held out hope, he occasionally fantasized about his true parents coming back to claim him. They never did, and the disappointment closed off his emotions.

He never had any real friends to speak of. He had learned the hard way not to get too close to anyone because they would likely not be around for long. So many people had disappeared from his life that he came to expect it - until Mama Sally.

He was arrested for being in the wrong place at the wrong time. He was under 18, and he was ordered back into the system, which he had previously run away from three times. The judge told him that if he ran again, he would be put in juvenile hall until he was age twenty-one.

Gordon was a star basketball player at his high school, which he managed to attend every day. Though he liked school, he had a reason to show up. He worked as a lookout at a dope house. When the guy who ran the trap house found out that he was a runaway, he took him under his wing, with one stipulation, he had to stay in school. He let Gordon sleep in the stash house and bought him clothes and food.

The coach spoke on Gordon's behalf when he was caught up in the bust. Coach presented straight-A report cards, and newspaper articles that credited Gordon for winning seasons and state trophies.

The reason for the leniency was that The Judge was a gambler, and one of his favorite sports was basketball. He hoped that the boy would make it without him having to enforce his threat to lock him up. He saw something in this boy that said he would go far if given half a chance.

The best friends that he ever had entered his life when he was sixteen years old. Clarence was twelve when he came to Mama Sally's, where Gordon had been for two years. That same week, Eugene - 10, and Paul - 8, arrived.

Gordon did not let his mentors down and got a scholarship to college. He got several full ride offers, not just because of his prowess on the basketball court, but because of his exemplary grades.

Gordon never forgot about his foster brothers, he spent his free time playing ball and helping them hone their skills on the court and academics. He brought them to visit with him during the summers when he could not get home from college. He paid for them to attend sports camps and paid for tutoring from the best available. He bought them clothes and did everything a big brother/father figure could. He was their go-to guy who was always there for them.

They all made it to college on scholarships and excelled in life. They were their own family and always came home to Mama Sally's every holiday, birthday, and milestone. They put their heads together yearly to create something spectacular for her birthday. They holidayed in Rome one year, something Mama Sally had always longed to do. The next year, they bought her a brand spanking new car, and the year after, they paid for a lot in a new development. All she had to do was pick out which model house she wanted and choose her color palette. They never failed to make her cry with their generosity. They were her boys.

Mama Sally was never blessed with children of her own, but she treated every child placed in her care as though they were hers. These four were not the only ones who remembered her kindness. Of the thirty-some kids that spent time with her they all said that she was the only person that ever made them feel wanted. When they were grown, they stayed in contact with her. There was always a full house during the holidays. She was front and center for weddings and the births of each of their children. She had a room at their homes and could come and go as she pleased.

That is why everyone was inconsolable when she died from a heart attack when she was attacked and robbed.

What the boys did not know until the reading of the will was that she had not spent any of the money that they had been sending her over the years after leaving her care. She had told them that she did not need anything but took the advice of her long-time friend and invested the money in computers and it had grown exponentially. The shares were divided among her wards and their children.

Mama Sally's attacker, while trying to cash forged checks was arrested. He received a lengthy jail term which most thought was not severe enough. Those who felt that way were visited by Mama Sally's spirit who told them to find room in their hearts to forgive. They got together and hired an attorney to get his time reduced and started visiting him in prison, it was what Mama Sally would have done.

In time he came to regret his actions. He kicked his addiction, found religion, and started helping others. When he was released, he moved into and helped run the foster home that was named for Mama Sally.

After graduating college, Clarence went on to play in the NFL. He was rolling in endorsements; you couldn't turn on the television or go ten blocks without seeing his face on a billboard promoting some product. He married his high school sweetheart, and they diligently worked on filling up their Long Island mansion with kids. He also adopted several orphans, and his charitable donations went into three shelters he supported.

Gordon did two tours and was a Navy seal recruited and groomed to step up and make the tough decisions when it came to defending the United States. He was currently studying for another degree while interning at the Pentagon.

Eugene graduated from a military academy and went directly into the Air Force and was in California training.

Paul was still in high school and was an MVP on the baseball team. If things went as planned, he was destined for the major leagues. He was a junior when Mama Sally died. Clarence stepped up to be his guardian. He went to petition the court and was declared an emancipated minor so that he could remain in Mama Sally's house. He did well in school and needed to stay where he was so he would not lose his footing. His brothers were always coming through to check on him.

CHAPTER 3
SHARILYN

S harilyn Thompson was starting her second year of law on a four-year scholarship. She had noticed Gordon in the halls and campus library.

Never one to be shy, she approached him one night, "I noticed that you are always in here late." Sharilyn said, referring to the empty library.

"I try to get into my study zone. I always did my homework at the library growing up. I find it comfortable here. I like it when there is no one around, it's quiet, I can focus better, and there are no interruptions," Gordon said abruptly turning his attention back to the book he was reading.

Sharilyn did not know how to take this. Was he dismissing her? Or did he simply not see that she was trying to start a dialogue with him? Or he wasn't attracted to her?

A lot of guys called her Marilyn because she had an uncanny

resemblance to the screen star, face, body, voice, and mannerisms. She talked in that breathy voice and had an innocent, naughty girl quality. With her hair dyed blond, no one realized that she was black, and she did not bother to tell them. The similarities stopped at visuals, she was a strong-minded, confident young woman – thanks to her parents and siblings who were ever present in her life.

The pastel cashmere sweaters and dresses that she wore over her full breast accented her small waist. No one would have guessed that she made them herself. Her mom had given her a toy knitting machine when she was ten years old, and she had gotten hooked on the craft. In her teens, she saved up and bought a professional knitting machine. She took lessons and joined a knitting club that met in the Cerritos mall. Soon her mom was selling her creations at her job at IBM. When she was fifteen, she opened a bank account and started her own LLC called Custom Cashmere. After studying every night, she pulled her knitting machine out and worked until the rhythmic sound of the knitting guide raking back and forth with every completed row lulled her to sleep.

She combined her creations with retro skirts, pants, and jewelry that she discovered while combing through resale shops. She saw every Marilyn Monroe feature. As the actress always said, "It takes a smart brunette to play a dumb blond."

Since Sharilyn had enrolled in the college many of her friends were white because there were not a lot of Black people on campus. She was allergic to athletes, having had her heart broken by one in high school. She had all the Black friends she needed back home in Compton, California.

Sharilyn made her way to a table on the other side of the room and unpacked her books. "It will be a cold day in hell before I speak to his bougie ass again. He ain't that damn fine. "I'm lying, yes he is," she said to herself.

Gordon was a nerd. So why was she so pissed? Being rebuffed was not something that happened to her. Though she tried to stop herself, every few minutes she glanced over her book at him, not once did she catch him looking back.

She could not concentrate and gave up on trying to study and made her way back to her dorm only to find her pillow and blanket sitting outside of the door. This is where she would be sleeping tonight.

Her roommate, C.C. was entertaining – something she has done a lot lately.

She could count on one hand how many times she had placed her roomie's pallet outside the door in the last two years. She had two boyfriends since coming to college, The first was eight years older than her and lived downtown in a loft. They spent time at his place or a hotel. He said he was too old to be sneaking into a college dormitory.

The second was a student and it did not take her long to realize that campus romance was not for her. Who wanted to keep running into an ex every day? Awkward! So why then was she so curious about the guy in the library?

She made her pallet and lay down in the hallway. It did not take her long to fall asleep and since Gordon was the last thing on her mind, she dreamed about him. They were making love, and she was calling out names, it didn't matter because she didn't know what his was. "Trevor, Lance, August!" He was a wonderful lover who did everything she would have had she been able to clone into a male version and make love to a woman.

Sharilyn heard laughter that did not fit with the erotic nature of her dream. When she reluctantly opened one eye, she was annoyed and embarrassed to see her roomy and the new boyfriend, along with two other girls staring down at her. She turned bright red realizing her hand was between her legs and she was in the aftermath of an orgasm.

"What in the world were you dreaming about?" C. C. asked between giggles.

"Nothing, girl stop being silly," Sharilyn said wondering just how far she had gone in her slumbering fantasy.

C. C. kissed her boyfriend goodbye, "Didn't sound like nothing to me, girl you were calling out names. Little orgy action going on in your subconscious?"

Tammy said, "You know in my psychology class they say that sex dreams are an indication that you are going without."

C.C. helped her gather her things up and take them inside the room they shared.

"Shut up Tammy, between you and C.C. enough sex is being had to fill the whole dorms quota," Sharilyn said.

"Jealous much?" Tammy asked.

"Don't get salty with us because you ain't been getting it in. Your coochie is probably covered in cobwebs," Julie commented.

"Don't worry about my love life and why does it smell like sex and ass in here?" Girl, you need to open the windows and spray some air freshener and wash that stank off your ass," Sharilyn said.

"We not talking about love, ain't nobody walking down the aisle. We just want you to enjoy the complete college erotic experience," C.C. said.

Sharilyn countered, "The only experience I am going to get this week is studying for midterms, and I suggest you all do the same."

"You are such a fuddy duddy," C. C. said.

"There is a frat house party tonight and I will be coming by for you at nine. Have your party poopin' ass ready," Julie told Sharilyn, who did not say anything before closing the door in her face.

The day was a long one, she was carrying a full scholastic load and had no trouble keeping up. She had always breezed through scholastics; this was attributed to her photographic memory. She retained everything she read the first time. She had a brain like a computer. She finished her last class and was loitering with some friends when she saw Mr. late-night library, she asked, "Does anyone know that guy over there?"

"He's in one of my classes, Gordon something," her flamboyant-gay-male-friend, Georgio offered. "He is the strong silent type. Girls fall over themselves trying to get his attention, but he never takes the bait. Though I know he is not playing on my team. I could not get that lucky."

Georgio dressed to the nines and was known for his prowess in doing hair and makeup. His mom owned a spa and salon in Hollywood. By the time he turned eighteen, he had a cosmetology license. He helped Sharilyn with her hair and make-up and she in turn taught him how to knit on an ancient machine that he found on one of their antiquing weekends.

CHAPTER 4
GORDON

Though Gordon was very attractive he was impervious to the effect he had on others. He had grown up listening to older players in the neighborhood who said that it was safer to deal with professionals until you decided to look for wifey material. At least a pro was not out to trap you and play games with your head.

The few women he had dated were duplicitous, transparent, clingy bitches looking for husbands. He didn't blame them for being on a mission, but their desperation frightened him. Very few made it into his bed. He would drop them off at the end of the evening and go home or to a fast house or contact a call girl to get his rocks off.

He rose early every day for his run and was at the gun range by five. He stopped for breakfast at the same restaurant every morning for the special. No other place made him close his eyes and see his Mama Sally through his taste buds.

The old woman who owned the café knew when someone appreciated her cooking and had his breakfast waiting for him every morning. Often, she sat down and joined him. Today was very busy and he would have to settle for examining the other patrons and profiling their lives.

The party-hard college crowd came here for something to soak up all the alcohol they had imbibed. Three raucous guys entered and sat in the booth in front of Gordon. His ears perked up at the conversation they were having.

"Man, this is going to be good, I have been jerkin' my gherkin' to fantasies about her all year. She won't give me any action. I nearly ran out of potion offering her drinks in hopes of getting her upstairs. She would accept the drink and carry it around for a while, then put it down without taking so much as a sip."

"Her mom probably warned her not to take candy from strangers."

"You were probably drooling so hard that she could tell you were a perv trying to dose her."

"Well, my wait is over, as soon as she drinks this coffee it's time to have a little choo-choo."

The waitress brought the coffee and Gordon watched as the young man added some powder and stirred. Moments later he noticed the girl who had spoken to him at the library come in and join their party.

The guys hunched one another as the girl sipped the coffee while studying the menu, impervious to the fact that she was about to be a victim.

Gordon beckoned for the waitress and asked for a to-go cup, "Well this is a first, you want me to tell Harriet to make your order of food-to-go too."

"No, just the cup will be fine. After you bring it, I need you to call the police, tell them it is urgent, and get here asap."

When he received the cup he rose, approached the girl, took the cup from her hand, transferred the contents into the paper cup, and put the lid on. The boy opened his mouth to speak, Gordon put his hand up, "Don't you say one word, the contents of this cup are going to the lab, after we identify which narcotic she has been dosed with to render her helpless so that you and the three musketeers can take advantage of her, your asses are going to jail."

When Sharilyn realized what Gordon was saying she turned to Mike and slapped fire from his ass.

Gordon held his hand out for Sharilyn, "Please come with me. I am sure the police are going to need your statement."

Mike tried to get up from the table and Gordon pushed him back down. He pointed to the three guys in the booth who were about to come to their friend's rescue and growled, "Don't move."

The cops came rushing in and Gordon relayed what he had witnessed and gave them the evidence in the paper cup. He had Joan retrieve the videotape of the guy putting the dose into the girl's coffee. The police handcuffed and escorted the guys outside.

Gordon sat down with Sharilyn, "What is your name?"

"Sharilyn."

"I'm Gordon."

"You sure it's not 'Knight in shining armor?'"

"No, but you have got to be more careful about who you take a drink from. I heard them talking before you came in. I recognized you from the library. I had to put a stop to their shenanigans."

"Did you just say shenanigans?" she laughed.

"Yeah, not a cool word huh?"

"It's refreshing to know that someone still uses it. You can use any word you want as long as I am sitting here with you and not somewhere having a train run on me. Thank you, Gordon?"

"You are more than welcome; no more than any decent person would do."

"There aren't many of them around."

"You just have to look."

The room started to spin for her, "I don't feel so good," she rubbed her temple.

"I was afraid of that, you ingested the drug, stay right here."

As he passed by Joan, he asked her to take an order of potatoes and some milk to Sharilyn, "Try to get it in her to help slow down the metabolization of the drugs."

He went outside to speak with the police officers who were searching the perps, "We are going to need an ambulance. They won't tell us what they put in her drink."

He grabbed one of the guys by his collar, "What did you give her?"

"All I know is that it makes girls agreeable. We only gave her a little," the boy was visibly shaking, "Please don't hit me."

"I'm not the one you got to worry about kid, wait until the guys in lock up find out that you are a rapist. They are going to love you."

"As soon as we hear back from the lab, we will know what to do to help her. We checked her vitals and though they look good now that could change. We are taking her into the hospital for observation," the paramedic told Gordon.

"Which hospital are you taking her to?"

"Mercy is the closest."

"I'll meet you there."

Joan had Gordon's food boxed up for him: "I put in an extra in case your friend gets hungry. She didn't have a chance to eat much before the paramedics arrived."

"Thanks, Joan. Do you have my check?"

"Don't worry about it, just go and help your friend. That was courageous thing you did. I'll be praying for her."

When Gordon arrived at the hospital the paramedic asked him, "Have you ever heard of Devil's Breath?"

"I don't know much about it other than the scientific name, Scopolamine. It renders the victim open to suggestion. Afterwards, that is if they survive, total memory loss. Overdose is common. I read one report where a New York man woke up to his penthouse stripped bare. When he went downstairs to ask what happened? The doorman said, "They loaded everything on the truck and drove it away." The man asked, "Why didn't you stop them?" The doorman responded, "Because you were helping them." They had wiped out his bank accounts and he had no memory of any of it."

"That's what they gave her. We are seeing more and more of this drug in the States over the last few years, it's nasty stuff. Women find out that they are pregnant with no memory of having engaged in relations, forget about trying to figure out who they conceived with, and there is a high probability that they contracted a disease."

"We need to find out how this is getting into the country and on the streets."

Gordon went to the desk and picked up the phone. He talked to someone who agreed that they needed to bring the guys into the Pentagon for questioning.

"You have stumbled onto something big Gordon, this shit is as bad as anthrax, if not worse. We have been putting a special team together to track it down. Do you know that you can walk down the street in Colombia and the plants grow like roses in America? How are we supposed to control something that is so easily attained?"

"I would like to stick around the hospital for a bit and make sure the girl is okay if that is all right with you sir?"

"Of course, by all means. I'll have the boys transferred here for questioning. You want in on this?"

"You know I do."

Over the next three days, Gordon spent his time going from the hospital to the Pentagon. It did not take long for the guys to give up their source who was in custody by the next day along with his supplier. They would follow this trail of breadcrumbs to the source.

Sharilyn's family flew in on a government plane that Gordon was able to provide with his commanding officer's assistance. He decided to put them up at his home where he had more than enough room.

He purchased a historic four-story house five years ago and spent all his free time renovating it. Once he had completed the updates no one would know that the house was almost two hundred years old. This 'painted lady' had been featured in several architectural and home remodeling magazines.

He had the fridge and freezer stocked. He hired two housekeepers to wait on his guests.

He knew that upon Sharilyn's release from the hospital, she would need bed rest. His home would be the best place for her to recuperate. The hotels were too sterile, and her family could not fit into a dorm room, his decision was the only one that made sense.

He spent hours by her hospital bedside because though she was for all intents and purposes out of the woods, the doctors did not know enough about this drug to say that the threat was over.

Sharilyn maintained her sense of humor throughout the ordeal. Gordon did not know whether the jokes were out of fear over what could have happened or relief that nothing had. Whatever the case, he liked it and found it easy to talk and laugh with her. He usually did not share about his life, but it was different with her. Once he opened up, he could not stop. He loved the way she listened.

Sharilyn could not imagine growing up as an orphan, "I admire you for being so strong."

When her family showed up it was like a stampede coming down the hallway. They wanted to talk to the doctor first and then Gordon for details.

Of course, they fussed over Sharilyn incessantly, but that was their way of loving her. Had one of them been in this situation, she would have behaved the same way.

Gordon found himself hemmed up in a corner, her brothers wanted to know where they could locate the fools that made the mistake of fucking with their little sister. He assured them that the perpetrators were currently being dealt with.

After Sharilyn fell asleep Gordon called for cars to take the twelve people to his home. The housemaids helped them settle in and served dinner.

Gordon sat with Sharilyn's mother, Diane, her sister, Marilyn, and a sister-in-law, Judith. They asked how he had met Sharilyn. He explained the details.

They looked at one another, "You mean you never spoke to Shar' before. Why have you gone out of your way to fly all of us in and let us stay in your home when you two aren't even dating?"

"Well, we aren't dating yet, but one can hope," he joked.

"Well, we will make sure that your hopes come true. You are a good man, and I will make sure that my daughter knows it. Where are your parents?"

"Technically, I don't have any. I was an orphan."

"That's a crying shame," Mrs. Thompson said shaking her head. "Who raised you?"

"Foster homes mostly. I had a nice foster mom in the end though, a wonderful woman, Mama Sally who took me in. She more than made up for what was lacking in my life."

"Any siblings?"

"Kids that I grew up with in Mama Sally's are my family."

Gordon could not help but realize that sitting around this dining room table with this family was a lot like it had been at Mama Sally's.

CHAPTER 5
SHARILYN

A week had passed since her release from the hospital. She was feeling fine and could not believe all that Gordon had done for her. She knew that she was in love, perhaps she had that syndrome where women fall for their rescuer. Now she had to figure out how her hero felt about her.

Her family had albeit given him their stamp of approval. She had not seen much of him over the last week. She and Gordon stood at the curb waving her family off to the airport.

"I enjoyed having your family here, I'm going to miss them."

"I appreciate all you did for us."

He looked down into her beautiful eyes admiring her long natural lashes, "You are welcome."

"Well, I guess I better grab my things and get out of your hair."

"What's your hurry?"

"No hurry, I just don't want to wear out my welcome."

"That's not possible, plus you are still supposed to take it easy."

"I'm getting behind in my studies."

"You can study here. I've made arrangements with all your professors. You are fine. You can make up your finals when you want to return to school."

She did not know what to say, so she said nothing.

"Hungry?" He pulled her into his arms.

"Famished," she wrapped her arms around his waist.

"Wait right here, while I lock up the house."

They went to a nearby bistro and ate Italian under the stars on the patio. They laughed and joked into the early morning as they walked through the park.

From that day on, they were exclusive. When they were not at his place studying, they explored the cultural and historical sites that D.C. afforded or jumped on planes to exotic beaches.

Sharilyn never moved back to the dormitory. They spent their weekends traveling around purchasing furniture to fill the house. When the weather was good, they spent their days in the garden and poolside, barbecuing with their circle of friends.

Sharilyn went home at Thanksgiving sporting a two-carat engagement ring and her fiancé. Her family was overjoyed. Gordon had her father and brother's blessing before they had gone back home after their first meeting.

It was a sunny day, and the couple lounged in the backyard waiting for the coals to get hot enough to grill steaks when Gordon asked her, "Do you want to move to California when we get married so we can be close to your family?"

Sharilyn squealed with delight. She could not think of anything that would make her happier. She had wanted to ask him about this but did not think it possible with his job.

"What about your work?"

"I have an opportunity to transfer to Long Beach, California."

"That would be wonderful. Do you think you could transfer in time for the wedding in June?"

"June? It feels like you are in a hurry before you seem to avoid setting a date, you said there was no rush, why the change now?" He rose to put the steaks on the fire.

Because I would like to be married before the baby comes."

Gordon was standing in front of the grill when her words sank in, he dropped the plate that held the steaks.

Sharilyn laughed at the expression on his face, "You know you just dropped our dinner on the ground?"

She was beginning to worry because he was not moving, it was as if he were in a trance. She rose and went to him, "Gordy are you alright?"

She picked up the steaks and put them on the grill, "Five-second rule, the fire will kill any germs," she joked.

She took his hand and led him to a chair. He moved as if he were a robot. Suddenly he burst into tears. This was not what she expected. She got up the nerve to cradle his head in her arms, "Baby tell me what is going on. What are you thinking? Are you mad at me?"

Gordon was embarrassed. He had never cried in front of anyone in his entire life, and here he sat blubbering like a baby after saying, "I'm sorry."

"Sorry for what? I am the one who should be apologizing. It was that night we did not use a condom behind the Lincoln Memorial. I forgot my diaphragm. We were caught up in the moment of lust. You know if we must, we could get this taken care of."

"Do not say that. Do not even think about it. You know where I come from. I'm delighted that you are pregnant. I have dreamt of being a father my whole life. I am going to be the best father this world has ever seen. One who sticks around and raises his children, not like my parents. Do not ever talk of getting rid of a baby. I couldn't live with that."

"I just meant that we could wait."

"Wait for what? This is God's gift. We are going to be wonderful parents, and I am happy. When did you find out?"

"I wasn't sure until a few minutes ago." She pulled a home pregnancy test from her pocket and placed it on the table. I have been ill every morning for the last couple of weeks. My mom called me this morning, she dreamt about fish, which means that someone is pregnant. She said she checked with everyone else, so it had to be me. She was right, as usual. She can always tell when a baby is coming. When my brother's girlfriend got pregnant, she told her before she knew herself."

"I am going to have to thank your mother. You must think I am crazy sitting here crying like this."

"Real men, cry. I'm happy too. More like 75% happy, 25% scared."

"Lots of people have done it, what are you afraid of?"

"Lots of people go into labor and don't survive or something is wrong with the child. There are dozens of things that can go wrong."

"We are not going to think that way. We are good, honest, God-fearing people. We are going to leave these things in his hands and trust and believe that our children will be healthy."

"You are right, I am focusing on events that are not real when I have no control over anything. I forgot that I am not running anything. God has my six."

"That's right," he kissed her long and deep.

"Baby, what if something about this mess they tried to drug me with could be in my system and hurt the baby?"

"We will cross that bridge when we get to it. I don't believe karma works that way, but if those fools did something to my child, they would have to deal with me. I do not want you to think like that. I want you to be confident in our Lord. There is no reason for our child to be stigmatized by those knuckleheads' actions."

"See you can say that shit, you ain't the one that is going to be running around all swole up, and you don't have to deliver," she punched him playfully.

"Baby, I will be with you every step of the way. You will not be alone."

"What if you are traveling when I go into labor?"

"We will be in California with your family by then. When the time is near, I'm going to take paternity leave. After the baby is here the government has day care centers so I can take the baby with me every day."

"You sure are going fast, don't you think that I might want the baby to stay home with me?"

"Who said you are going to be at home? You did not go to college all these years to sit at home. There are a lot of lawsuits that you must win. Did you decide on what branch of law you want to specialize in?"

"I have. I am thinking about family court. I want to do something that will help children that cannot help themselves, not just letting gangsters and dope dealers stay on the street because I found a loophole or paid off the right Judge."

"That is so like you, always looking out for the underdog. That is why I love you," he kissed her on the neck.

"Watch out now! You better go turn them steaks over, you're going to need your protein after dinner."

"And you are eating for two."

"Since we are talking about jobs, are you ever going to tell me about yours?"

"Well, how do I put this? I investigate aliens that are a potential threat."

"You mean terrorist?"

"Yes."

"Is it dangerous?"

"Well, I do more technical and computer research. Now and then I find myself in the field but that is what bulletproof vests are for."

He did not think it a promising idea to let her know that he was often in the thick of the fray, but there was so much that he could not tell her. Even if he could, he would not, because he did not need her stressing while carrying their child.

"If it gets dangerous you would tell me, right?"

"It will not. Can you please set the table and stop worrying?" He kissed her on the forehead and turned his attention to the steaks.

When they went to Compton for Easter Sharilyn and Gordon broke the news about the baby to both their families at a combined dinner that they hosted.

The couple was out for a walk after dinner when they happened upon a house that Sharilyn had been in love with since she was a young girl walking this way to elementary school. They looked at one another and without a word agreed. They took the 'For Sale,' sign as a good omen. He paid in cash; no mortgage would burden his family.

The house directly behind theirs came on the market the next month and on impulse Gordon purchased it. Sharilyn thought it would make a great rental property, who knew when a family member might need somewhere to stay? It could be a gift to their firstborn.

They made the huge indoor/outdoor kitchen the hub of the house. It all came together quite nicely on paper. They agreed that family dinners would host the two families. They had enough room to accommodate everyone.

The kitchen would make any restaurant proud. It had all Lynx professional grills, warmers, and appliances. You could grill, fry, make pizzas, or have a seafood boil or rotisserie a twenty-pound turkey. Three subzero refrigerators. Built-in couches, tables, and bars made sure that over a hundred people could sit comfortably.

Four big-screen televisions housed in custom cabinets to protect them from the weather made this the place to be for sports games and fights. It was the heart and soul of the two properties. The kitchen opened onto an enclosed wrap-around patio that housed a custom-made table that seated one hundred people easily. Automatic sliding doors led into the integrated pool area that had a bar where people could eat and drink. It looked much like an extravagant resort pool with waterslides.

The women put their heads together and started making wedding plans. Sharilyn would have a combination baby shower/bachelorette party weekend at an ocean-side Malibu spa. Sharilyn graduated with honors and two weeks later was married at her family church.

The D.C. house was leased to visiting officials, through a government agency. Gordon transferred to the Long Beach office. He traveled to Washington D.C. once a month to report to his superiors. At home, he worked from nine to five.

Sharilyn's family was a big part of Gordon's attraction to her, he loved that they were always around. He did not want her to lift a finger. They moved in with her parents while he, with the help of her brothers and friends, renovated the houses. He was adding a second level and the pool, complete with a separate guest/pool house and covered patio. The outdoor kitchen brought the two properties together.

They went to the doctor and though they said they did not want to know the sex of the child until it was born, they had not said anything about the number. Gordon was jumping up and down like a kid on a trampoline when the doctor showed the twins on the ultrasound screen.

Gordon went to work the next day bragging and beating on his chest like King Kong. His friends and colleagues were happy for him. He was the last holdout of all his fraternity brothers. All would be front and center for his bachelor party. His military friends from around the country had reserved seats on military flights.

Clarence arranged the festivities. They had the top two floors of Caesars' Palace in Las Vegas. To say a fun time was in store for all would be an understatement.

When the children were born, they named the boy Gordon Jr and the girl Gloria. The next year came a set of twin girls, Sharice, and Clarice. Two years after that came another set of boys, Jason, and Joey.

Gordon spent as much time as he could with the kids. He went to work at 5:00 in the morning so that he could pick the kids up from school and get them to their extracurricular activities. He coached football, baseball, basketball, and soccer. He was the Boy Scout troop leader.

The girls had drill team, ballet, modern dance, track, drama, gymnastics, and singing lessons. Gordon printed out a schedule every week so that they could keep up.

Sharilyn took care of the girls' gymnastics and ballet on the weekends. During the week she worked at the courthouse where she had worked her way up to the Defense Attorney's office.

Before they knew it, they were celebrating their sixteenth wedding anniversary. They could not have been happier - Until…

CHAPTER 6
GORDON

G ordon was looking for VHS tapes of a meeting about agreements and laws in the archives. He found the file he was looking for and while replacing the box, another fell. It was a sealed box that was so old that when he picked it up the bottom came loose. As he picked up the papers and returned them to another box he discovered a videotape with no label. He took the tape so he could look at it and label it later.

He put the tape in the video player in his office. He had to watch it four times to figure out if what he was seeing was reality or someone's idea of a joke. Government officials and aliens were planning a shelter that would house one million people while Earth regenerated itself. Regenerated from what?

He spent the next few weeks in the archives searching for more unlabeled videos. He found one, it was a meeting where the officials told the aliens that they would acquiesce and help with their plan. The last part of the tape discussed how they would use natural disasters to whittle down the population before the big day when they would use nuclear weapons to clear the planet.

What could he do about this? For obvious reasons the powers that be had left him out of the loop. They could not trace his genealogy. From what he understood, the government was planning to deploy weapons from globally positioned satellites, wiping the planet clean of all human and plant life. In the ocean, chemical bombs would bring the ocean water to a boil, killing off all the mercury-filled fish and marine life cleansing the water, much like you would if shocking a dirty swimming pool. In a year they planned to repopulate the ocean with cloned marine life mass-produced in the shelter aquarium. They were going to kill everyone, except a chosen few, who would live in the shelter for three years until it was safe to come out.

His job for the last eighteen years had been to make up histories and identities for alien relocations. He thought they were from other countries, not other planets. He made sure that they melded into society and adapted to the communities.

Gordon had taken a military vow, and he knew that anything he did, and anyone he told, would jeopardize their lives as well as his, not to mention treason. He knew why the population needed to remain ignorant, but now they were talking about screening out people, Thinning the herd as if they were cows. What did this mean for his family? No mixed races, no diseases, no humans over thirty years old, only the purest of the pure.

It would take two years for the wind and rain to wash away the harmful chemical residue so the planet could begin to regenerate itself. In the third year, scientists will assess the environment and when everything is all right the population can emerge into a clean world with no pollution or diseases.

Gordon had to figure out a way to protect his family. When he went home that night, he sat in his office researching on his computer. He found out where they were building shelters. A Dallas, Texas and a Los Angeles, California sportsplex was under planning. They would be the perfect places. There was one other option, but it was in Japan, a building with a huge indoor beach, but the location made it unlikely, he would focus on Dallas and Los Angeles.

Gordon sat on the computer for hours. He turned on a radio broadcast that they had been monitoring for years, Art Bell - A radio personality with a large following. The government had kept a close eye on him and for good reason, his broadcast warned that there was extra-terrestrial life among us, and to think, they had convinced all but a handful of the population that he was a quack.

Gordon went back to the archives and discovered three tapes that he needed to review. The aliens did not know that the security cameras had taped their private meetings. From what he could surmise, the government did not know that the aliens were only keeping humans around for reproduction purposes and slave labor. They decided that they should include African Americans because as slave labor they were a strong race capable of working long hard hours in heat or cold.

Gordon knew that the only people who knew were supposed to know. People who became a threat became dead. He also knew that he was a threat, even though he was inadvertently a part of the conspiracy. He had kept their secrets and done his work like a good military agent. If they found out that he knew, they would kill him. He could not save the world, but he could save his family.

There were a handful of colleagues that he trusted. Once he explained that they were not going to survive this they had no choice but to help him come up with a solution.

He would have to work fast. He did not know how much time he had to implement the plan that was germinating in his mind. On the drive to work he mentally started putting the pieces together. By the time he arrived, he had phoned five people and woke them out of their sleep. He wanted to make sure that they would be available to meet him at 1:00 in the afternoon at a hotel near the job. He would meet them in the bar after getting a suite. Then he would feel them out before taking them upstairs to view the tapes.

The first thing Gordon did at work was go back to the archives. He took an empty box that he would duplicate for the sealed box, this accomplished he went back to his office and began checking his messages. He went through the boxes and read every note and scrap of paper. He put an employee directory into his briefcase so that he could track the cyber addresses and research each party. He scanned each page. Copied the videotapes and secured a locker at the post office where he would keep the originals.

He printed out a list of all the files where he had archived information about the aliens for whom he had created false identities. He needed to know where they lived and worked.

On his way-out Gordon informed his secretary, "I'll be taking the rest of the day off."

He had discovered that two of the people he had called this morning were in the loop. He called them, "Hey Marty, looks as if I am going to have to reschedule our meeting. One of the twins is sick. I am sorry about this, but I will get with you tomorrow, all right?"

"You sure it will wait? I mean you woke me up at dark thirty in the morning, and you sounded a little spooked, you know that can be contagious. Why don't I come by your place after work?"

"Tell, you what, let me go and look into this situation and I'll let you know, maybe I can meet you for a beer later, sound good?"

"Sure, I'll talk to you then."

Gordon realized that Marty and Jefferson had both been on a fishing expedition. They were suspicious. Good thing he had not said anything over the phone this morning.

When he arrived at the hotel bar, four colleagues were already enjoying appetizers. He showed them a file filled with memos that spoke of a building that was in the planning stages. He divided the copies among them.

"It looks as though someone is building some sort of long-term shelter, but for what?" Shane asked.

"This one here says that they need at least a four-year food supply," Darren said.

"This is about global satellite positioning all over the world. And I am not sure, but these coordinates implicate that the targets are all densely populated cities," Kevin said.

"What's going on Gordon?" Yvette asked.

"Let us order and finish our lunch, then we can go upstairs. I have something you all should see."

"Man, you have got me spooked," Martin said and motioned for the waitress.

"Good," Gordon said.

They all ordered drinks and burgers with fries.

There was no conversation as they examined the documents.

When they finished their food Gordon asked, "Everyone ready to go upstairs? I took a suite so that I can show you all five videos that I ran across in the same box where I found these memos." Gordon beckoned for the waitress and gave her a credit card to pay the bill.

They all sat in the suite and watched. Gordon had not seen all the tapes; some he had found this morning and was viewing for the first time. Things were worse than he thought.

The tape was of the first meeting when the aliens had revealed themselves to the humans. That was back in 1971. The following videos proved that their plans were already underway. The last video ended.

No one spoke a word. They sat stunned. The only sound in the room was the ice clinking in their glasses as they drank from the bar that Gordon had forethought to provide.

CHAPTER 7
SHARILYN

S harilyn woke up at 3:00 a.m. And rolled over to an empty pillow. She rose and went to Gordon's office. She found him with his head on the desk snoring, she kissed him gently on the top of his head until he woke.

The look in his eyes alarmed her. "What's wrong, honey?" You did not go to the boys' game today, you did not come out of this office for dinner, and now I find you here asleep. This is not like you. It has been this way for almost two months now. Can you tell me what is bothering you?"

He pulled her down into his lap and buried his face in her shoulder. "I love you so much. I will do everything I can to keep you and our family safe. I must tell you some things and I hope that you understand and keep a cool head. Most important, I pray you will not hate me after you see what I am going to show you."

"Nothing could ever make me hate you, Gordy. You are my husband and the father of my children. Whatever it is I am still going to be right here by your side."

"You know how I have always told you that I could not discuss my work with you because I took a vow, a vow that I thought was important to keep?"

"Yeah, and I have always been all right with that."

"Yes, you have, and I love you for that. Honey, there are things that I am going to tell you now that you cannot discuss with anyone. If they ever find out that I know what is going on they will kill me and anyone that they think I may have spoken to. Do you understand?"

A chill ran through her, "You are starting to scare me, but yes I understand."

Gordon picked up the remote control and pressed play. She silently watched the video. When one ended, he put in another, until she had seen them all.

He turned it off. "My job is to place aliens among the population and make sure they have social security, department of motor vehicles documentation, history and identity. It is what I have done since I took the job with the pentagon only, I did not know they were space aliens, I thought they were other country aliens."

"I see," Sharilyn said. She had not processed what she had just seen. "O.K. let me get this straight, these ghastly creatures are about to take over the world and the government, and you have been working hand and hand with them. They want to kill everything on the planet, including me and my children, my family and friends?"

"I guess that's about the gist of it, believe me when I say that had I had a clue that these people meant harm to the world, I would not have been a part of this. I am trying to come up with a way to put a stop to their plans. Tomorrow, I mean in two hours when I go to work I am not going to work on the maintenance of their disguises but to discover who and where they are so that when the time comes we can get rid of them instead of the other way around."

"O.K.,"

"Don't you have anything to say?"

"No, not right now, maybe tomorrow after I think about it some more."

"Why don't you try and get some sleep, I have some more research to do before I go into the office."

"I don't think I can sleep, matter of fact I am going to have to take the day off. I'm going to have a drink, you want one?"

"No thanks, I have been hitting the Hennessey since I came home. I need a clear head to put a plan together. Try not to worry too much," he kissed her on the cheek.

"Yeah right, are you crazy?" She said as she poured herself a large glass of cognac. "You are telling me that aliens are going to wipe our asses off the face of the earth, but not to worry. Do you have any idea how I am going to feel walking around with this knowledge in my head? Not to mention that I am going to be wondering who is human and who ain't," she broke into tears.

"I was wrong to burden you with this." He pulled her close.

"If you had not warned me, I would have been extremely disappointed. If I got to go down it will be fighting, and you best believe, I will be taking some of them with me."

Come Monday morning; Sharilyn had taken a week off from her practice. Two years ago, she had hung the shingle for her law firm after being the District Attorney for the Compton Courts for more than a decade.

This week she was working hard, putting the final touches on the Manuel Dominguez High School, Class of 1977, 20 Year Reunion. She did not know what made her head the committee, she had a full plate between her business and family.

She had done a great job. The reunion was being held at the Hyatt Hotel in Long Beach. Friday night there will be a meet and greet in the hotel bar. The reunion is in the ballroom on Saturday night, and on Sunday there is a picnic at El Dorado Park.

Confirmations flowed in every day. The turnout would be much better than the ten-year reunion. Many of the alumni had gone on to do remarkable things. The class of 1977 had borne doctors, ball players, local business owners, musicians, rappers, authors, pharmacists, politicians and Government agents. She looked forward to seeing her old classmates.

In 1987 Sharilyn had heard that Claudette was in Hawaii working as a tour guide. Milton, Sharilyn's older brother had gone to Hawaii for his honeymoon and ran into her. The next day they got together for brunch at her apartment on the Ala Wai.

When Milton returned, he gave Sharilyn a present from her old friend, round trip air fare and an invitation to visit with her for two weeks. She moved some things around and six months later she was touring Oahu.

They had a wonderful time. Claudette showed her every tourist spot on the Hawaiian Islands. If she had not gone to school for so many years to be an attorney, and did not have a family to think about, she would have left it all behind to live in this paradise.

Claudette was proud of Sharilyn and told her so when they hugged goodbye at the airport. They stayed in touch by phone. Conversation flowed easily for hours as they caught up. Sharilyn was elated when she received a check from Claudette to pay to attend the 1997 Reunion.

CHAPTER 8
CLAUDETTE

laudette flew into LAX a week before the reunion. She had not been home in seven years. I was excited when we got off the plane and saw my father and son, Davonne, who was now nine years old. We hugged and cried.

They loaded the luggage into Clyde's van. When they pulled into the driveway, her husband Darrien noticed that the street was lined with cars, "Whose cars are these?"

"My family."

"But these are Mercedes and Jaguars."

"That's right."

"But I thought your family was poor."

"Why did you think that?"

"I don't know, when you said you grew up in Compton I just assumed."

"Property in Texas is cheaper than California, even though this house is a fraction of the size of ours it would sell for three times more. Most of my family are hardworking honest people with good jobs. There are truckers, real estate agents, engineers, beauticians, law enforcement. The ones that were gangsters are either dead or in jail. You never asked me much about my family, but you are about to find out right now."

Family poured out the back door of the house. I walked down the line hugging and kissing all my aunts, uncles, cousins, and friends while introducing Darrien and our children David and Chavonne. I looked around and suddenly realized that I had missed them. I started crying.

"What's wrong Claudette?" everyone asked.

"I missed all of you so much."

The way my family greeted Darrien overwhelmed him, he had never been hugged and kissed so much in his life. It took a while to get through all the introductions.

Inside the smell of Mexican food, which was Claudettes' favorite was enticing. Jo Ann, Phyllis and Francis had cooked everything including a German chocolate cake.

There were dozens of children that I was meeting for the first time. I sat for hours catching up with my family. I was so proud of them. David and Chavonne were having fun with their cousins. They ran around playing in the backyard, it did not matter that it was the middle of the night, there was a big light that made it as bright as daytime.

Hours later, everyone was leaving and had promised to return tomorrow for the barbecue, it was time to go to bed. We slept in my old bedroom which was now Davonne's. Darrien was already sleep; he had drunk too much Hennessey with the men of the family.

David and Chavonne were finally ready for bed, they had stayed awake so late because they had slept on the plane, "Mommy, are these people all my family?" David asked.

"They sure are baby. You ain't seen nothing yet, there will be a lot more here tomorrow."

"Are they going to be our cousins too?" Chavonne asked.

"Your cousins, aunts and uncles and lots of friends. You two had better get to sleep."

"Mommy?"

"Yes?"

"I like having a bunch of family, can we just stay here so that I can play with them all the time?"

"I do not think that your grandparents can manage that. Next Friday all the kids are going to spend the night with you, and you are going to have an old-fashioned slumber party, how about that?"

"Cool."

"Mommy?"

"Yes."

"They talk different, and say we sound funny."

"It is called slang or ebonics, don't worry you'll catch on soon enough, as long as you understand what they are trying to communicate you'll be alright."

She cuddled them into her on each side and they slept one on each arm. She began to hum and the kid's joined in as they did every night, "Hu hum a hum a hum hum."

It felt good being home, her bedroom welcomed her back after all these years. As she slept the room's memories crept into her dreams.

The next day Clyde, the grill expert, introduced Darrien to the two grills he had made from oil barrels set in wooden cabinets that he had built himself. Aroma poured from the smoker. By noon, the backyard was packed with people who had come to welcome me home.

Anna had gone to the senior care home to pick up Helen, her mother and Sadie, her aunt. I was taken aback at their frail physical appearance. I sat with Helen half of the day and in the afternoon helped my mother put them down for a nap.

I was busy with many of my friends who came to welcome me home after being gone for so long. Sharilyn and Yvonne were in touch with many of my home girls and had invited them to the barbecue at my parents' request. They arrived with a dish and a beverage.

The back yard was jumping with old school music floating from the speakers that faced outside from the den. By dark the party was in full swing. It was an old-fashioned garage party.

The next day my dad took me and the kids to visit his mother. She was in a home in West Los Angeles dealing with diabetes. We stopped at one of my favorite restaurants, Bills Taco House on Martin Luther King Blvd which used to be Santa Barbara. Bills was around the corner from the house his mother had lived in before she got too sick to be on her own.

My father had introduced me to all my favorite eateries. The best burgers in town came from a little shack on 54th and central, the place did not have a name they just referred to it as the sisters, because two sisters ran the place. There was always a line outside. The burgers had so much meat in them that you had to hold them with two hands. The news did an expose on hamburger joints and found that they made the burgers from horse meat. That did not stop the customers from coming though.

Then there was a restaurant on El Segundo and San Pedro where you could get a huge pastrami sandwich with a dipped bun. They cooked the thinly sliced pastrami meat in chicken broth and placed it on a toasted French roll with mustard and sour pickles.

The burritos from the place on Melrose could feed you for three days, and the burgers from Mom's place by Compton High School were lethal. I was going to have a fast-food feast while in California.

Darrien had to leave on Monday evening on business. He would be gone for two weeks and there was no way he could make it back in time for the reunion.

I visited with friends who came by and picked me and the kids up to go to their homes for a couple of days.

I was back at my parents one morning in the backyard on a blanket, I was reading a book to the children. A police helicopter circled overhead, suddenly a man with a gun in his hand climbed over the brick fence and ran through the gate. Seconds later two police officers followed in pursuit.

David and Chavonne had never seen anything like this and were not accustomed to the sound of the constant sirens. The only birds they saw in their back yard were blue jays and other Texas breeds. They knew nothing of ghetto birds and guns other than what they saw on television, and I wanted to keep it that way.

Wednesday night, my cousin Donald, who was a Los Angeles Marshall took me to a night club downtown. I danced the night away. The next day I stayed at the house resting up for the upcoming reunion weekend. I cooked and spent time with Davonne.

CHAPTER 9
CLAUDETTE'S
REUNION

I dressed for the meet and greet. When I arrived at the hotel bar there was a good crowd. I sat and caught up with my classmates. They all shared pictures of their children and other halves.

"I need a cigarette. Anyone want to join me outside?" Sharilyn asked.

Several people followed her out as it was illegal to smoke inside. They started singing 70's songs.

Sharilyn was feeling no pain thanks to four Long Island iced tea drinks, "Look, you are all my people, and I have to tell you guys something." She wiped away a tear. "Look, you all have heard about the satellites that they have been sending up into space. Well, they are not just satellites they are bombs. Aliens living among us plan to set off bombs to wipe the world clean. During this time, they are going to live in shelters where only a few chosen humans will be spared."

Everyone looked at one another.

"Look, I know y'all looking at me as though I have lost my mind, and I do not blame you. I would think I was crazy too. If y'all know like I know you need to build yourselves a shelter and get you some AK47's."

"Sharilyn, are you still getting high?" Carolyn teased.

"You can say I'm crazy if you want to, one day you are going to wish you would have listened to me."

They finished their cigarettes and went back inside. They drank and reminisced about the old days, "Claudette do you remember when you were on the homecoming court, and you were riding on the front of that Cadillac, and they started shooting?" Deborah asked.

"Oh yeah, that was fucked up. My daddy made that dress for me, it was blue."

"All you could see was that blue dress. Girl, you hit that chain link fence and flipped yourself over like it was not nothing," Sharilyn laughed.

"Chile, bullets ain't got no names on em, I was getting out of dodge."

"Claudette are you still sewing?" Zenia asked.

"You know it, she stood up and modeled the blue suede pantsuit that she was wearing.

"Girl that is fly, you made that?" Carolyn asked.

"I have been specializing in mommy and me clothes to lately."

"Girl I still have that recycled jean suit that you made for me, I can't fit it, but I still got it," Beverly said.

"Yep, you guys remember modeling my designs in the fashion show?"

Girl that was a lot of fun and we got to go to the other schools and model," Zenia said.

"We met all the fine Niggas," Sharilyn said.

"Girl, I married one of them from Compton High," Carolyn said.

"Girl, you married that guy. He was good looking," Claudette said.

"And had two kids with him," Carolyn said.

"So, is he coming tomorrow night?"

"Naw girl, he died three years ago."

"I'm so sorry, what happened?"

"He got the virus. We separated when I found out he was gay."

"Are you alright?"

"Oh, I am fine. He did not get it until after we broke up. The kids were five and six. Towards the end his health was really going downhill. I let him come home, by then the kids were fourteen and fifteen. It was hard for them to deal with their father when he was out doing his thing, but when he came home, they made their peace with him. I even forgave him. The fact that I had wished he was dead when he told me he was gay made me feel kind of guilty, but the life insurance made me feel better, me and the kids are fine, and I opened my little clothing store with the money."

"I'm glad you are alright."

"Hey, maybe you can make up some pieces and put them in my shop? We can make some money girl; you know the recycled thang is back in style."

"Sure, that's a good idea."

"Ya'll need to come visit me in Texas. I get lonely out there, but you know I got to stay where the money and my man is," I said.

"By the size of that rock on your finger it looks like he's taking good care of you," Patricia said.

They talked about their friends who had died during high school. It seemed that every month there was a funeral to attend thanks to gang warfare.

"Hey, you guys remember Bartenders funeral?" Henry said.

I stood and picked up my champagne glass and poured some of my drink onto an empty bowl, "For those who ain't here."

Everyone stood up and followed my lead. They went around the table and said a name of a person who was gone and how they died before pouring a few drops of their drink out.

The bar was about to close. We went to an after-hours joint and partied for a while.

I was drunk and so glad to see the bed where I stayed all day nursing a hangover. I did not get up until it was time to dress for the reunion. I wore a black and gold sequin gown.

The hotel lobby was full of alumni checking in. They had the usual chicken for dinner, and everyone was called up to speak on the mike and tell them what they had been doing for the last twenty years. They gave out awards. I received the award for 'The person who traveled the farthest.'

The band geared up and the party started. We danced to the Ohio Players, Earth Wind and Fire and Smokey Robinson. We did the hustle, the bump, the worm, the point and the freak until the hotel put us out of the ballroom.

We went upstairs where we reserved a block of rooms on the ninth floor. We left the room doors open, and people floated from room to room. We tuned the radios to the same old school station and had a Soul Train line going down the hallway.

It was five in the morning when I got back home. I was worn out and ready to sleep so she could get up by noon to attend the picnic.

Chavonne stirred, "Hi Mommy."

"Hi baby, what are you doing woke?"

"I wanted to hear about the party, I tried to wait up for you, but I fell asleep."

"Well, come on and lay next to me and I will tell you all about it, until we fall asleep. Tomorrow we are going to a picnic, and you are going to see all the people that I went to school with."

"Why can't we go right now?"

"Because I had so much fun and danced so much tonight that if I don't get some sleep, I'll be too tired."

"O.K. then you go to sleep now, you can tell me about your party tomorrow on the way to the picnic."

Chavonne patted Claudette on the back and they hummed themselves to sleep. "Huhum, a hum, a hum."

CHAPTER 10
CLAUDETTE BACK HOME

I had finally started to garner some interest from publishers for my first book, 'The Roux in the Gumbo,' which debuted in 2005 with a vanity publisher. When that two-year contract was up I decided to self-publish and put out five more books.

I spent months helping my uncle, Willie Bruce Jr. clean up "The Kings of Credit," which he had written while on a state-paid vacation for more than a decade. He had also studied and learned to write movie scripts.

Willie encouraged me to turn my novels into movie scripts. I had dreamed of my family attending the red-carpet premiere of my movie at Grauman's Chinese Theater.

After taking Shaundra Rhimes masterclass it was not long before I realized that I did not get the same flow I did while drafting novels. The words seemed to flow through my mind and through to my fingers onto the pages and before I knew it, I was typing, "The End."

No matter how hard I tried I felt like I was not doing my ancestors justice. I decided to stay in my own lane and pay someone to write the scripts for me.

I was a member of "Black Pearls Keepin It Real Book Club which had just celebrated their twenty-third anniversary It was a few years before I found someone who I felt could do my ancestral history justice. Brian W. Smith, born and raised in Louisiana, had over thirty books and I hired him to write my movie script. He had just premiered his movie Premonition and was on his way to the next one.

I traveled to literary conferences, attended library signings and book club conventions and was invited to attend and speak at several meetings where my novel was featured as book clubs read of the month. I also made my gumbo for several meetings and word spread.

I used a large chunk of the book money to remodel our home, something that I had wanted to do since we moved in three years ago. A pool and two thousand square feet were added to the two-story house that sat on three acres. I wallpapered my office with the rejection letters that I had received over the years to remind me of how far I had come. In the center of the wall was a framed copy of the acceptance letter and literary contract with the check stub of my first advance.

I had just come off a book signing tour and was on the list for Oprah's book club. My birthday was coming up in a month and I wanted to do something special. called a travel agent and booked airline tickets for twelve of her home girls to visit for a week.

I could not wait for the six weeks to pass when they would arrive.

I arranged for four limousines to pick my friends up from the airport. When the cars arrived there was only Sharilyn, Yvonne, La Juana, Zenia, Deborah and Wanda.

"Where is everyone else?" I asked.

"They were supposed to meet us at the airport and never showed," Zenia said.

"I spoke to them last night, what could have happened? Those heifers could have told me if they were going to flake out."

"I tried to call Deborah Greene and did not get an answer."

The drivers brought their bags into the house. I showed them to their rooms so they could freshen up and change into their swimsuits and unpack. I attempted to phone the six who had not shown up with no luck, except when I called Sarah's house.

When everyone came down to the patio, they all looked worried, I was crying.

"What's up," Lawanna asked.

"Sarah is dead."

"What did you say?" Yvonne put the plate she was making from the buffet down.

"Sarah is dead, someone broke into her house and killed her. Her mom answered the phone, the police are there right now."

"I just had lunch with her and Myrene yesterday," Wanda said.

Claudette went into the kitchen and got glasses and a bottle of champagne and a bottle of cognac. They could all use a drink.

David walked into his sister's bedroom and changed the television channel, "Chavonne look, aren't these mommy's friends?"

"Yeah, I remember them from California."

Chavonne picked up the phone and dialed her grandparents to make sure they were all right.

"Whatcha doing?" David said.

"I'm calling to see if grandma and granddad are alright."

"Good idea."

They went down to the patio and turned on the big screen television, "Mommy look."

They were all taken aback in horror at what unfolded on the screen. Channel four was showing pictures of people who had been found dead this morning.

They looked at one another as they heard the names of their classmates, including the six who had not made it to the airport and twenty others. They were all graduates of Manual Dominguez High School, class of 1977. The news had no clue of how they died or what connected the victims.

"What the hell is going on?" I asked.

"I called and grandma and grandpa are alright," Chavonne said.

Sharilyn called her house and got a recording saying that the phone was out of order. She tried to reach Gordon at his office.

"We need to warn everybody," Wanda said.

Sharilyn called Alison who was a classmate who lived down the street from her house, "Alison you have to be careful someone is going around killing everybody from Dominguez class of 77.

"Sharilyn is that you?"

"Yeah."

"Oh my god, Sharilyn, are you sitting down? Because if you're not you need to."

"What's going on?"

"Sharilyn I was just down the block at your house watching them take a body out. We all thought it was you, but it must have been your sister. Sharilyn, your house was blown up. There is nothing left where your house was but a pile of rubble. Your brother went to the school and picked up the kid's they are with him, and no one has been able to contact Gordon."

"I have to go, Alison be careful. I think you should leave town for a while. Just get on a plane and leave."

Sharilyn hung up and dialed her brother. "The kids are fine," he said knowing that would be her main concern.

When she hung up, she burst into tears. Everyone went to her and when she could get the words out, she relayed what she had just heard.

Darrien walked in and he stood not knowing what to say since he did not know what was going on. David filled him in.

"Dad what are we going to do? Are we safe?"

"Don't worry son, we'll be alright." He sat and listened to the women.

Sharilyn phoned Gordon on his cellular phone, "Gordon are you all right? What is going on?"

"Thank God that you are alright. Your sister is dead. This is the government. Sharilyn this morning I got an email it was from a Kinko's address; I think it came from Marty; he was trying to warn me."

"Warn you about what?"

"Sharilyn, you said something at your class reunion. You warned people about the conspiracy. The government doesn't know who you talked to, so they are killing everyone who was in your class."

"Are you serious? Oh God, this is my fault?"

"I am afraid so. I was checking something out in the shelter and when I was coming back up, I heard your sister scream and an explosion. All I could do was close the shelter door to save myself."

"Oh my God, what are we going to do?"

"Sharilyn I am standing here looking at what used to be our home. There is nothing left."

She didn't know what to say, her sister was dead, and her husband could be killed at any moment.

"Look I am going to get the kids and your family members, and we are going to fly out to Texas. You need to contact as many of your classmates as possible, tell them what is happening. I must go now. You stay safe, I will call and let you know when our plane lands."

"I will have Claudette help me make some hotel and car arrangement."

"Good idea. I love you."

Sharilyn hung up and told the others what was happening. They all got their cellular phones and started calling the alumni.

Darrien could not believe what he was hearing. He went to his office and called his cousin who was in the Navy.

His cousin told him that he would call him back as soon as he did some investigating.

Sharilyn had the list that she had compiled when she was sending out the invitations for the reunion. She asked Darrien to print out the list and she gave each of them a page with phone numbers and they all got out their cell phones and started making calls. About every half hour the news would interrupt programs to tell of someone else who had been dead. They also said that the connection between each victim was that they were all from Manual Dominguez High School, class of 1977. They urged any graduates to get to the police station for protection.

They were on the phones for hours. I called everyone in my family and told them to be careful. Darrien booked a private flight for my family members. They would arrive that evening.

My uncle Eugene was in a group called the Black Underground which was affiliated with Art Bell. He had information that confirmed everything Gordon had said. "I have been telling y'all for years about these aliens and y'all thought I was crazy. I am going to come down there and we can work together to try and stop this, meanwhile I am going to put y'all in touch with the underground members who live in Texas. You are a target and will need them for protection."

I called my cousin Tracy who was a postal truck driver running mail from Los Angeles to San Francisco, "Girl that shit sounds crazy to me."

"Crazy or not, Tracy all you have got to do is look at the news and call me back."

Tracy stopped for lunch and in the café, she asked the waitress to change the channel, and the regular broadcast was interrupted with the news about the murders. "Damn my cousin is part of that class and she just called me saying that this shit is all connected to some kind of government plan to kill everyone on earth, and they are going to stay in some shelters until it is safe to come out. Meanwhile everybody else is going to be dead," Tracy said to some truck drivers she knew who were sitting at the counter.

"Hey if that shit is true, we have got to do something to stop this," one of the truckers said.

"Oh, it's for real all right. I got a call from my wife yesterday. My son's wife who is black was in the class of 1977, my boy found her, and he is in a bad way. It is like he lost his mind or something. I am trying to make it back home now, I remember that weekend when they came back from some Alumni get together and they came home drunk and were telling me and the missus about their old friends and they were making fun of a girl who was talking about this very same thing."

"One of my friends has a son who just put the plumbing in their backyard for a lead shelter they built. She was not just jerking their chains," another said.

Tracy picked up her cell phone and called Claudette back, "You now have my full and undivided attention. I am sitting in a diner with a man who has just lost his daughter-in-law, her name was Sharice Johnson."

"Oh my god, I knew her."

"We looked in the mail I picked up today, there are a gang of letters from the government. We just opened some of them and they are letters about an important meeting, the recipients of this mail are select-ed to go into the shelter you talked about."

"Bring a few of them and maybe we can get someone to imper-sonate a couple of them and attend that meeting," I said.

"I will be there tomorrow, I already talked to my mother and my sister, they think I'm crazy, but they also think the stuff on the news is scary, so they are packing now.

"I'll have transportation waiting for them at the airport. See ya cuz, be careful."

"You too, I love you."

The doorbell rang and I went to answer. Ten guys pushed past me into the house without saying a word. They all looked like Black Panther's from the 60's era, with their afros and black leather coats. They also had a huge trunk that they carried inside. One of them carried a gun with a silencer on it, and something that looked like a kid's space-ship. Two of them were holding up a man in army fatigues, he looked as if he had just had the living daylights beat out of him.

I was really afraid, my friends came and stood by my side won-dering who these thugs were.

"Who the hell are you guys, and what's wrong with that man?" Zenia said.

"Who is Claudette?" one of the men asked, he was in charge.

"We are with the Black Underground, your uncle Eugene called us and just in time, if we had not gotten here when we did, you would all be dead."

Another guy stepped forward with the toy. This guy was sitting down on the block, he had this remote control and when we grabbed him, we took it from him. We pushed a couple of buttons, one marked 'return' and out of thin air this thing flew back to us. It has some kind of cloaking ability, we need somewhere that we can, he put his fingers up and bent them as if to say quote, unquote, question this guy and a loud radio to cover up any noise he might make."

"Are you guys going to interrogate him? Can I watch?" David said excitedly.

"Tell you what little soldier, why don't you show me to your room, and we can figure out what this thing does. Are you familiar with remote control toys?" Alfred asked.

"Am I ever, I have a remote-control robot, and a bunch of cars."

"Let's get to work then, you don't want to watch him get interrogated, it's not going to be pretty, plus we have to find out what this thing does and quickly."

"Let's go up to my room." David led the way.

"We can take him out in the garage if you could move any cars out. I picked up my set of keys and tossed them to him. "Keys for the H2 and the Lade are on there."

"I sat on the stairs with Chavonne on my lap. I could tell that she was terrified. afraid. That child had not missed a beat, she heard, saw and comprehended everything. I took her upstairs to her room so that we could talk.

"Mommy, are we going to die?"

"We are going to do everything we can so that we do not. You scared."

"A little bit."

"It is alright to be scared, mommy is scared too, but you know what? Scared just means you are smart enough to watch your back. The good thing is that we know what they are up to, and they don't know we know. You don't ever have to be afraid of dying, we don't want to volunteer to die either, so if we do, we are just going to have to make sure that some of them go with us, right?"

"I guess."

"If we do die, that just means that we go and be with God. Remember your Awana lessons? You have got to be brave; we are going to do the right thing and whatever happens is in his hands, understand?"

"Yeah, what can I do?"

"I'll let you know when I know, but meanwhile why don't you come and help mommy cook, we have a lot of people to feed."

They went down to the kitchen and while her homegirls were still on the phone trying to organize things, they started cooking. Darrien went back to the grocery store and two of the Black Underground went with him for protection.

I went outside to smoke a cigarette and saw that there were about twenty Black Underground outside the house. They all had on long black leather coats, and I knew that my neighbors would get suspicious. It was the middle of July and would soon be a hundred degrees or better. There had to be another way. She went back in the house and went to the garage to talk to Malcolm. When she opened the door, she was a bit taken aback at what she saw. They had the guy that they had brought into the house stripped naked and strung up. He was bleeding from several cuts, both eyes were swollen shut and he had what looked like electrical wires connected to various parts of his anatomy. Malcolm saw her and got up and walked into the house. "Malcolm, I live out here in La La Land and we are the only Black folks. What do you think these White people are going to think when they see twenty men walking around in the yard with them coats on as hot as it is? "

"I see your point," he laughed.

Malcolm went outside and spoke with the men. Several of them got in their cars and left. He noticed a 'For sale' across the street and took out his cell phone and called the number on the sign. He arranged to meet with the realtor in an hour.

He went back into the garage and picked up the soldiers' wallet. "Cool and the gang, a platinum American Express card, here you go Samuel, why don't you get on a computer and start ordering some things that we are going to need to secure this house and the one across the street. Get in touch with Alex and tell him that I need him to come and meet the realtor. He has got to get us to that house as soon as possible. Tell him that it is empty, and the price is seven hundred grand. Joe, you ride around the neighborhood, get the numbers for every house that is for sale. We are going to have to house a lot of folks. Find out where the closest apartment buildings are and get everyone filling out leases. Meanwhile find the closest hotels and book up a couple of hundred rooms. Tell them that it is a convention and the people we had made arrangements with fell through and we have to put something together fast."

I stood in the door listening, "I have a friend, Ann she works for Wyndham hotels, she could get us some good rates and we can book some ballrooms for meetings."

"Call her, let her know that folks will be checking in as early as tomorrow, think she can swing it?" Malcolm said.

"Shit, once I tell her what's up, I'm sure she will jump on it with both feet."

"G.I. Joe is singing like a bird, that fool didn't know what was up. Now that we have started putting his information with ours he wants to be down with us, he says that once he talks to the other brothers at the military base, seeing as how they would be crossed out too, he knows he can get a bunch of snipers and explosives engineers on our team, what you think?" Herman said.

"What if he crosses us?"

"If he crosses us, he crosses his dam self, his pigment is as dark as mine. That means he is going to die. Joey's out there showing him the proof right now, he was black before he was military and he got a

White wife and mixed kids, he wants to call them and get them out of his house just in case they figure he done flipped the script, or went AWOL," Herman said.

"Give him a Cellie and let him make the call," Malcolm said.

"He has to be hurting, should I run him a bath with Epsom salt? Maybe it will take some the pain out of the cuts. I have some aloe vera, maybe by the time he gets out of the tub his wife can patch him up with some poultices soaked in herbs," I felt bad for the guy who had just been blindly following orders, especially since he was not trying to kill me anymore.

"I'm a doctor let me look at him," Zenia said as she walked into the garage.

"Sure, good looking out, I'll have Joey hook him up with some morphine after he gets in touch with his family, it's going to take at least a couple of days to put him back together," Herman said.

Darrien's brother Devin was scheduled to come to town that day on business. With all the excitement I had forgotten all about it until he was pushed through the back door flanked by two of the Underground. They both had him by the arms and a third was going through his briefcase. "What is going on here?" Devin asked. They shoved him into a chair.

I heard the familiar voice and hurried into the kitchen; I could not help but laugh at the flustered look on his face. "Hold up, that's my brother-in-law."

"Claudette what is up here? Who are these men?" Devin said as he picked up the papers that had been strewn over the table. At that moment Darrien walked in the door carrying groceries followed by four others.

"Devin, how are you?" Darrien asked.

"Freaked the fuck out, again I ask, what the hell is going on here?"

"Why don't you come outside, and I will try to explain as best I can, I don't know much, but what I do know is not good."

While they were outside, the other men returned, they rang the doorbell, and several black suburbans were parked on the front lawn. They were unloading all kinds of computers, televisions and video cameras. There were ladders strapped to the top of the cars. "What is all this?" Sharilyn said when she opened the door, and they started bringing in boxes.

"Security."

When Darrien and Devin came back in, they started helping them connect all the computers. Several were outside mounting cameras. In each window they connected automatic weapons with sensors and remote controls.

"This shit ain't going to go off and start killing my neighbors while they are out for their evening walk, is it?" I asked.

"No, they won't shoot unless we want them to. Don't worry all these men are trained soldiers, most of them are ex-marines, cops and CIA, DEA, and FBI. They all know what they are doing," Herman said.

The doorbell rang and Yvonne walked to the door and opened it. The geekiest looking guy you ever wanted to see stood there. "Can I help you?"

"Is Malcolm here?" he said in a high squeaky voice.

Malcolm, hearing his name, came out of the kitchen. "Hey, Alex, what's up rich boy."

"Got the papers for the house across the street right here, the sooner we get these babies filled out the sooner we can get in, since the house is empty the realtor said that he could lease the place to me until escrow goes through. We could be the owners as soon as next week," Alex said.

"Get busy then, Darrien can you get him on a computer?" Malcom asked.

"He can use the one I just set up in the bedroom at the top of the stairs. What is he going to do?" Darrien turned to the short man, "You look awfully familiar to me for some reason."

"What business are you in."

"Telecommunications."

"Well, if you stay up on your computer science you may have seen me in a few papers or on television, I…"

Darrien interrupted him, "I know who you are. You are the CEO of one the biggest selling computer programs in the world, you are Alex Hamilton."

"Guilty," Alex said.

"Alex here is one of the biggest hackers in the country, if they only knew all the back doors that his program has. There is not a company that does not use his software for one thing or another and he can sit and scan every business, not that he needs the money or anything, but he just likes to keep a finger on the pulse. That is how we found him. He found out about this plan and contacted some people who were associated with some folks who knew some people, and he and his money have been a big help." Malcolm said.

"Well, it's an honor to have you here, Mr. Hamilton." Darrien said.

"Alex, please."

At that moment Joey came back, he had a list of each house that was in the neighborhood with a 'For Sale' sign in front.

"We need more houses, and it seems like most of these are re-altered by the same man, a Bob Grissom." Malcolm said as he read the list.

"I know him." Darrien said.

"How cool is he?" Malcolm asked.

"Well, if what they say about excluding anyone with an illness is true, Bob would be eliminated because he suffered a bout with cancer last year. His wife is Filipino, so she is not eligible. For some reason she can't have any kids, and they have adopted several, it looks the rainbow tribe over there." Darrien said.

"We need to go and feel him out, can you arrange it? Call him and tell him that your associate wants to look at some houses out here," Malcolm said.

Darrien took Alex to the room at the top of the stairs. He checked his bank info on the computer. Lloyd glanced over his shoulder, he had never seen so many zeros in one account in his life, he wanted to cry.

Darrien reached Grissom who said that he would meet them in half an hour. He went into his office and did a search on realtor.com. He printed out each one that looked like it would fit their needs. The fact that the entire area is zoned for acreage was a plus. That way your neighbors were not up your butt and in your business. He often said that houses in other communities were so close together that you could open your window and pee in your neighbor's toilet.

Lloyd loved the house that they lived in. They had started look-ing for property when his ship came in. The lot they looked at had a pond in the middle of it and Kim said that she did not want to deal with the critters that came with a pond. She was still shook up from the snake that she had seen next to the pool at their home in Plano. They were heading home discussing why he wanted it, and she did not, when they stumbled upon this development, as they rode through a man was putting a 'For sale' in front of the beautiful two-story house in a cul de sac. He could still hear her excited voice, "Pull in there Darrien, that's our house."

"What do you mean that's our house? You are crazy."

"Just stop, please." She jumped out of the car and as she viewed the backyard she beckoned for him.

"You can't just go into someone's yard like that Kim."

"Darrien you have got to see this, you know those trees you said you wanted, they are right here."

Reluctantly he had gotten out of the car. It looked like a park behind the house which sat on two acres. There had to be at least three hundred trees beyond the manicured lawn. She was right, this was their house, he liked it. "This is nice."

Claudette had noticed a calming look spread over his face, the last time she had seen him look so serene they had been in Jamaica without the kids, and it had taken him four days to get out of work mode and attain this aura. "I want this house, this is our house," she said.

The rest is history, they moved in five years ago.

Malcolm, Alex, and Darrien met Grissom on time. They looked at six houses. Grissom almost had a heart attack when Alex turned to him and said, "I want all of them."

"What do you mean?"

"I mean I want to buy each one of these houses."

"You can't be serious?"

"Yes, I can."

"What do you want with all these houses?"

"I have a big family and want to move them close to me."

"Well, I guess I had better make some phone calls. Let me give you the paperwork so you can get started on it."

Darrien was impressed. What must it feel like to be able to purchase six houses that were over half a million dollars at one time without blinking an eye? It had to be a wonderful feeling.

Back at the house, David ran out to greet them. He was excited. "Dad, Dad, we figured it out."

"You figured what out."

"You know, the flying killer saucer."

Malcolm explained, "When we caught G.I. Joe he had a remote control in his hand, it was directing a drone that you would not have been able to see until it was too late. It has a clocking device programmed to search for a person. The laser will render them helpless and then it injects them with poison. After that it explodes. That baby had enough liquid explosive to level your whole lot. You would have all been dead without God's grace and us stumbling up on him."

"I don't believe that this is happening."

"And the government wants to keep it that way."

"What do we do next? What if there are more of these things flying around?"

"Dad, we are making a device that will confuse the signal that it uses to identify people. We took apart the remote and rewired it. All these drones work off a satellite relayed signal, all we need to do is hack into their program and confuse the directives. Instead of it being able to seek a target, we can direct them to return to the sender and explode."

"A boomerang effect. This is a smart kid; it was his idea. Now we need Alex's help working out the details and we better get on it quick, because in the last hour the police have found ten more bodies." Alfred said.

"Frank's wife is here." Joey said.

"Who's Frank?" asked Malcolm.

"G.I. Joe, remember the military man?"

"I think you should let us prepare her to see him. You all messed him up bad," Yvonne said.

"I guess it would not be a good idea for his kids to see him either, maybe we should move him to a hotel and his wife can go with him. You know this is not a safe place for him since this was where they sent him and if they check and see this place still standing, they are going to know something is up." Malcolm said.

"The kids should definitely not see their father like this. Let me talk to her." Yvonne said.

Yvonne approached the woman and introduced herself, she found out that her name was Cheryl Ann. She was soft spoken and appeared to be in her late twenties. Her children looked to be about the same age as Claudette's, they stood at her side obviously curious about all the activity.

"How about we get the kids settled in and then we can talk."

"I guess so, where is Frank?"

"That's what we have to talk about, why don't you have a seat in the den."

Yvonne went into the kitchen where Claudette, Chavonne, David and Zenia were marinading ribs and steaks. "The marine's wife and kids are here, and we need to go and talk to her. Chavonne and Lloyd Jr. I need you to take her kids up to your room and watch a video or something. Do not tell them what is going on. Can you manage that?"

"Yes," Chavonne said.

"Sure," David said. The kids went into the den and introduced themselves to Frankie and Shaquan and invited them to go upstairs. The boys headed for the Xbox in the upstairs den and the girls went into Chavonne's room.

"Hi, my name is Claudette, and this is Zenia. Yvonne said your name is Cheryl Ann?"

"Yes, can I see my husband now? Is he here?"

"Yes, he is here, and you will see him shortly, but I just need you to bear with me for just a little bit longer so we can try to explain what is going on."

"O. K." Cheryl Ann said resignedly.

"Your husband is hurt. Zenia is a doctor, and she has taken care of his wounds, and assures us that he is going to be fine."

"Oh my God, where is he? What happened? I must see him right now."

"He was beaten, he has some cuts and bruises, we have given him something so that he can sleep, in a couple of days he should be up and around, but it is going to be a while before the swelling goes down, I don't think that you want the kids to see him like he is," Zenia said.

"Who did this to him?" At that moment Malcolm walked in from outside. "I am afraid it was my men, but it was because the white man had him doing their dirty work. Actually, our finding him before he blew this house up with Claudette and her family in it was a good thing. That is why you are here."

"Oh god, are my children and I hostages? Are you guys like the Taliban or some political group?" Cheryl Ann shrank back as she asked.

"Naw, Naw, nothing like that. We are trying to save lives; it is the government that is trying to kill everyone. Look, I have some things to deal with, but they will explain everything. Please know that no harm will come to you or your children, at least not by our hands. Your husband will be fine, I guarantee it," Malcolm said and patted her hand reassuringly.

Malcolm went into the kitchen. "Yvonne, Frank has called some guys from the army base, they should be here soon with their families. Direct the kids upstairs, the men into the garage and the wives with you. I need the women to explain what is going on to them. Cool?"

"Sure. Look, we are not going to be able to cook the amount of food we are going to need in this kitchen. Can you get your men to go and pick up some grills, you know the kind with burners on top, big ones?" I spoke.

Malcolm's stomach growled as he remembered that he had not

eaten since early morning, the meat was not cooked and yet it smelled good. "You ain't said nothing but a word, dang that food is smelling good. I will have them get right on it."

The doorbell rang and Yvonne went to answer it. There were eight marines standing there with their wives and kids. "Come on in. Kids go upstairs, husbands go in the garage and wives in the den."

Claudette got up and went into the kitchen, she put several bottles of rum, cognac, wine, and champagne along with plastic cups on a portable bar and filled an ice bucket and rolled it into the den. Yvonne and Tricia followed her with plastic chairs they had gotten out of the garage.

The women came in, and saw Cheryl Ann. They all knew each other because they lived in a military housing community. Cheryl Ann told them, "Franks injured, they have not allowed me to see him. They say these people beat him."

The women were standing in the den looking in horror at the events that were unfolding on the television. They wondered if this had anything to do with why they were here.

"O. K. ladies make yourselves comfortable. I know that it is early in the afternoon, but if the spirit moves you, help yourselves, the bar is open," Claudette said.

"Please, I would really like to see my husband now," Cheryl Ann said.

"I think that you should wait just a few minutes, that way we can let your husbands explain what is happening to everyone at the same time."

Suddenly Cheryl Ann was not so soft spoken anymore. "I don't give a rat's ass about what's happening, do you think that I can hear a fucking word that you are saying, I have got to see my husband right now," she shrieked.

"Why don't you let her see her husband? I will tell her whatever she needs to know later," Alice said.

"Come with me Cheryl Ann," Zenia said as she placed bowls of chips and salsa on the table.

They went into Claudette's bedroom where Frank was sleeping. She walked to the side of the bed, her breath caught in her throat. She placed her hand on his swollen cheek and his eyes fluttered open.

"Hey Ann, are the kids here? They are all right? he asked drowsily.

"They are fine Frank, upstairs playing. What about you, are you all right?"

He grabbed her hand, "I am going to be fine; it looks worse than it is. Do not worry, we are going to be fine thanks to these people. Cheryl Ann I was a fool, they were using us. They ordered me to kill the people who live in this house, kids and all and I was going to do it because they told me that they were part of the mess in Iraq, I believed them. After they have us killing off all these people, then you know what they are going to do? Cheryl Ann they are going to kill us, they are going to kill everybody," his eyes closed, and he fell back to sleep.

"Why is he talking out of his head like that? Who is going to kill everybody? Is he crazy?" Cheryl Ann asked.

"Believe it or not, he's telling the truth," Zenia told her.

"Oh my god, what is happening?" she asked.

"You come on back in the den where you can get the whole story. Frank is going to be asleep for a while. That is the best thing for him right now." Zenia put her arm around the girl's shoulders and led her back into the den.

Sharilyn was explaining what was going on. Cheryl Ann went straight to the bar and poured herself a large Hennessey, she threw it back in one swallow.

"Cheryl Ann, you don't drink hard liquor," Alice said.

"I do now, and if I were you, I would have one before she starts telling you what's happening, trust me girl, you are going to need it."

"How is Frank doing?" Sylvia asked.

"Well, I have seen worse. His wounds are just some bruising, swelling, and small cuts, but the things that he said, I thought that he was loopy from the medicine, you know being a nurse I see it all the time, but Zenia said he is telling the truth. Oh my God, Claudette I am so sorry, and he is too, I can tell, even though I do not know everything. Frank would never hurt a flee unless it was to protect his country. He said that they lied to him. Oh my God, when I think of what could have happened, your beautiful children, Oh my God. Do you all realize that they are sending our husbands out to kill innocent United States citizens, kids, mothers, and fathers? Can you believe all this is happening right here in America?" She stopped talking long enough to down another drink. "Those bastards are going to kill us all. Don't you see? They send them out to murder folks and then when they are through with our husbands they are going to kill them too. And us. Not just them but everybody," she said and poured herself another drink and tossed it back. Her speech was getting slurred now.

Alice stood up and led her to the couch. "Come on honey, let us sit down over here so we can all find out what is happening. It must be something serious because in twenty years I have never seen you drink like this."

Alice and Cheryl Ann had been friends since junior high, they both met their husbands when they were stationed in North Carolina for training. They had been married in a double ceremony and their children had been born within days of each other. Alice was worried about her friend.

Sharilyn told the whole story as Gordon had explained it to her, the tapes, the aliens, the news reports corroborated the murders. Before she finished talking, they were all drinking.

When their husbands came in the house they went outside to talk to their wives, they laid blankets on the grass and each man confessed that over the last week they all had been given orders to assassinate people. Some had already completed their missions. That very morning Alices husbands' superiors had ordered him to Michigan to kill a family.

"I could not do it; the man had a wife and kids the same age as mine and they looked like such a happy family. I came back and reported that the man was not home. If they knew I lied I could be court marshaled or killed for not following orders, but I could not do it." Shane said.

"I completed my assignment two days ago and I have been having nightmares ever since, I keep seeing the house blow up, I ain't been able to sleep or eat. Now he knew that these people were not criminals or terrorist, but civilians that should never have died. I do not know how I am going to live with myself. And knowing that they are planning to kill us, we need to find out who is behind all this and knock them off." Jason said.

"We do not even know who they are? Sharilyn said her husband will be here soon; he has been helping these people blend in for over twenty years now. He can help us find and illuminate some of them, but what will that get us?" Hamm said.

"Yeah, that satellite bomb is going to go off, there is nothing we can do about that, we have a few years to figure out how we are going to survive, now that we know what they are up to." Richard said.

"I called the base and told them that Frank had a car accident, that way when it is time to go back to work next week, he won't have any problems," Harry said.

I have an idea about what to do about some of the targets, we get some corpses, put them in cars and houses and blow them up. We get the real targets plastic surgery, new identities, and history. Since I am the one who programs the drones, I can target whoever we need taken out instead of the citizens.

Those of us who have assignments need to give the names to Malcolm. Lots of targets will be arriving here in the next few days. We will simulate their deaths. Some we do not have to worry about because I can make those drones so hot that there are not even ashes left to sift through. When we first started using the drones they were just to hunt and kill, but they wanted to clean up the mess at the same time," Addison said.

"Too much press is watching. This way there are no bodies, but as sloppy as they are, I do not think that they are concerned about people finding out who is behind this because in a couple of years or less they are going to kill everyone anyway," Jesse said.

"I was going to sign up for another tour, I don't know about you guys, but in three months I'm out, but while I am still in, I am going to cause a lot of accidents," Hamm said.

All nine of these men had enlisted together. They had been in the marines for ten years. They had known each other since grade school in Los Angeles. They were all members of the same chapter of the Crips. They had watched their friends die in drive-bys and gang wars. Those who were not dead were in jail, they realized that if they wanted to live to see twenty, they had to do something different. When Hamm's brother, Sampson came home on leave he had talked to them about the benefits of the military, he made it sound so good that when they graduated, they all enlisted.

They had been there for each other through wars, natural disasters, 9/11, weddings and births, through thick and thin. They were not going to be played and used by the government anymore.

Three suburbans pulled up and the men started unloading the grills. "Hey, we could use some help over here," Joey called. The marines went to give them a hand.

"Maybe we should go in and help with the food," Alice said.

"This is so beautiful. You know I never even knew any of these developments were back here. I have a sister who lives right down the road in Allen. We come out to the stables in Wylie where she boards her horses. I would love to live out here," Jenna said.

"On our husband's salaries, are you kidding?" Alice commented.

"Hell, we are married to hitmen, they should be able to ask for a raise, at least some hush money," Jenna walked into the kitchen, "What can I do to help?

"Are you ladies alright?" Claudette asked.

"Not really," said Cheryl Ann as she picked up her glass of Hennessey that she had left on the counter, "My husband is a... What did you call them Jenna?"

"Hitman."

"Oh yes, my husband is a hitman, the government is about to wipe everyone off the planet including me and my children. I am standing in a house my husband was ordered to blow up with your whole family in it, all of this," she spread her hands wide and in doing so her drink flew out of her glass. "Oops, my bad." She hiccupped every few seconds and you could see the little birds that must be flying around in her mind's eye like an animated cartoon character.

"I am sorry, but I must tell you that I don't understand shit you are talking about. You may as well be speaking Greek or some shit, it's me, or maybe the Molly I just took?" Sylvia said. "Don't look at me like that, this is a lot to process."

"You got any more?" Lillian asked.

"I don't have Molly, but I got some kick ass weed that I grew,"

Deborah put a box on the table and started grinding up the marijuana and rolling joints. Sylvia sat down to help her.

"Cheryl Ann it could be this moonshine that got you blabbering and slurring your words." Alice said.

"Girl that Hennessey is the bomb. Anyway, as I was saying, all of this would have been ashes, and do you know what?" She stumbled over to Claudette, crying now, "I am so glad that those men caught my husband and whipped some sense into him. I would like to kick his ass myself," she slurred and burst into full blown boo hoo's.

I pulled my new friend into my arms, "Things are going to be fine one way or another, God has our backs."

"I do not believe that I am accepting all this generous hospitality from the woman my 'follow-orders-without- questioning- husband was going to annihilate, and should say God has my six, it's military jargon." She giggled.

I put my arms around the drunk girl and said, "He did not know what he was doing. All of your husbands are going to be a great help to our cause, which is survival, they are right there under the people who are giving these orders noses, now that they have been clued in they can get us more information, why don't you come with me? I'll get you something comfortable to wear and you can go and lay down with Frank for a while, we will wake you up when the food is ready."

Cheryl Ann put her hand to her head. "Maybe that's not a bad idea, you know I never drink anything stronger than a wine cooler, and all this yack is going to my head. Is the room spinning?"

I led her away, and Yvonne and Zenia got the others into the kitchen and gave them green onions to cut up and a pot of boiled eggs to peel to go into the potato salad. They talked as they prepared the baked beans and cole slaw and made hamburger patties. They had a ton of food to cook.

The men were outside setting the eight grills up and bonding. The Black Underground members and the marines were brainstorming on a plan. They had decided that the best thing to do would be to get people jobs on building the shelters that they were passing off as sports-plexes. They could infiltrate and take them over. There was no way that the detonation the aliens were planning to set off could be stopped, but they could make sure that their families were inside and safe, instead of the ones who were behind this conspiracy.

The Black Underground had taken off their leather coats and put down their automatic weapons since the cameras were set up and they felt they were safe since the marines had called and reported that Frank had partially completed his mission by killing Claudette." There was nothing else they could do right now but come up with a plan to thwart the enemy.

"I told them that Frank was discharged from the civilian hospital but could not report to work for at least a week. The officials said that no further action was necessary at this time," Albert said.

The Black Underground had also bought some outdoor lounge chairs and four kegs of beer and blenders to make margaritas. They might as well loosen up will waiting for the others to arrive so that they could finalize plans.

CHAPTER 11
GRISSOM

G rissom called and requested that Alex go with him to the title company. He had gotten on the phone and made the offers to the owners. He researched Mr. Alex Hamilton and was so excited with what he had discovered that he danced a little jig. This was going to be the biggest payday of his life.

Each homeowner was extremely happy to accept the offers that were way over the asking price on the contingency that they move immediately and throw in the furniture.

Grissom felt that something was going on and when he arrived at Darrien's house, he knew that his suspicions had been accurate. There must have been two hundred people milling about. "Having a party Darrien?"

"Not exactly, come on up to my office we need to talk. I have done some research, and we believe that it would be in your best interest to be in on this." Alex handed him several documents pertaining to the conspiracy. After he looked them over, Darrien started the videos on the big screen television.

Grissom sat down in a chair and started reading, he sat silent for several minutes,

"This is some sort of game, right?"

"I'm afraid not, have you been watching the news today?" Darrien asked.

"Are you referring to the murders of the class of 77?"

"My wife is in that class and they sent a marine with a drone to kill us, all these people here are involved in an organization that knew about the government plans, the others are marines who were carrying out orders, but now that they know the real story they are on our side." Darrien said.

"So, you're saying that the United States government; along with aliens from space, are planning to kill off all the black people?" Grissom asked.

"Alex handed him more papers, "Not only Black people. The sick, mixed races, only people that they designate will prevail, and not many of them because there seem to be a couple of million aliens. As you can see from that paper your recent illness and your wife's nationality makes you ineligible."

"Even if I was eligible, I would never go along with such a diabolical plan," Grissom said.

"So, we can depend on you for your help?" Lloyd asked.

"I'm in, and I know a lot of others who would be interested too. I also know the developer for the sportsplex, he has an Asian wife. So why are you really buying all these houses?"

"We need a place for all these people who need protection to stay, and we have some military families and the Black Underground and we are talking to other organizations to help."

"Well, here are the keys for the house across the street. I have some storage units with abandoned furniture that you can use. I have four houses on the other side of Winningford Road. They are not fancy, but they are big. Two of them have guest houses. I will give you the keys to the storage and the houses as soon as we come back from the title company.

Other houses I can write up as rentals. Two of the houses you just bought are owned by army friends of mine. They were both good soldiers who were wounded in the war. I'll call and invite them over. You show them what you showed me. They would be a tremendous help."

Grissom and Alex left.

Darrien went outside, the marines were standing over the grills with beers in their hands. Someone had brought out a boom box and it was set on an oldies station. He picked up a beer and sat down for the first time since this fiasco came to light.

Devin came out and sat next to him, "Lynn doesn't believe me, but she is getting on a plane with the kids, she will be here in a few hours. I just got accustomed to having a family and the thought of this conspiracy makes me realize that I could lose them in the blink of an eye. That woman in there, Sharilyn has just lost her sister, it was supposed to be her, and they are hunting for her husband. This is some scary shit."

"You are telling me; I would have been ashes if it were not for Malcolm and The Black Underground. We must realize that we are just living out God's plan and according to Alex we are going to come out on top."

Darrien's sister came up the walk trailed by Larry, one of the Black Underground, carrying her sleeping daughter six-month-old daughter, Laura. Devin took Laura from him and went into the house to lay her down in Chavonne's bed.

Darrien handed Larry a piece of paper with the address, codes and keys to the storage unit located around the corner. "You are going to need a truck. Get everything, we have six houses to furnish."

"Sweet," he said and turned to walk away. "Hey, Darrien can I speak to you for a second?"

"Sure, what's up?"

"Well, they say that you are one of those computer brainiacs and looking at this spread you got here, well you seem to be a pretty smart guy, what's your take on all of this?"

"I still have not figured it out, but I definitely believe that we are in danger and have to protect ourselves. I am grateful for you all showing up when you did. I hate to think of what would have happened, but God must be with us, right?"

"He's always with us, but that doesn't stop me from being scared shitless."

"I know what you mean."

"By the way, is your sister married."

"No, are you?"

"I lost my wife four years ago. I was in the Drug Enforcement Agency for twelve years. I took down a big mafia kingpin, got him locked up for good. He reached out and sent me a message. They shot my wife and two-year-old daughter. They were getting into the car coming home from the grocery store. Well, you didn't need to hear all that, but no, I'm not married and if I were to ask her out it would be the first time I have had a date since they died. But I figure with the fact that we may not make through this, she might be a nice person to try and get to know."

"Hey, good luck. Did they ever charge the man with your wife's murder?"

"No, but if they had it would not have made any difference, he already had life. I got myself put into the prison and took care of him myself."

CHAPTER 12
DARRIEN

A t seven in the evening several people disembarked at DFW airport. Most of them had come from California and were Claudette's family, some were the class of 1977 with their families. His family would be coming in from London and Jamaica.

All of them were scared. There were Limo's waiting for them. Some rented cars and headed for Claudette's house. Her parents, uncles, aunts and cousins were on the flight with her friends. When they arrived at the house it was almost nine at night. They were all eager to find out what was going on and what they could do to help.

They all went out into the back yard and Malcolm and Gordon explained everything. Darrien had gotten an inflatable outdoor movie screen, and he played the videos for everyone who sat on blankets, tables and chairs that Darrien had rented. They watched as they ate dinner.

Gordon had arrived and explained how he had discovered this diabolical plot.

Gordon had everything he needed to make identification for everyone. "Any one with computer experience can work with Alex, he will show you how to build history's; previous job, medical, social security cards, ancestors, siblings, birth certificates anything you can think of to make a new identity."

Bob Grissom and his army buddies were there, along with Franklin Kutcher who had the contract to build the sportsplex. Franklin had watched the videos and while they played, he realized why some of the specifications for the building seemed extravagant and unnecessary. He could not believe that he had not figured it out for himself. No sportsplex needed a whole twelve-mile green house and hundreds of thousands of small sleeping compartments.

He brought the blueprints on compact disc and Darrien brought up the plans for the sportsplex. "I will hire everyone that knows anything about construction or buildings to fill out applications after you have your new identities. They all had ideas how to make the sportsplex accessible for them and not the intended inhabitants.

I am going to need at least five thousand people, those who can be trained should come also," Franklin said.

"That's a good idea, then we can take over the building if we can't find a way to stop the satellites from going off and killing everyone." Malcolm said.

"Yeah, we can build it and up to the day that they are to go in we can set the doors so that they cannot get in and we will already be inside. Everyone can move here." Bob Grissom said.

"I have four empty rooms that I can let people sleep in, and I am sure that some of the neighbors would be willing to offer space, there is no one in this development who would make the list, they all have some kind of ailment or mixed heritage." Jim Dale from across the street said.

Bob started assigning housing, the Black Underground who were coming from all over the country would buy or rent houses in the area. They would set up headquarters in the house across the street which had a secluded backyard which would serve as their meeting place. At the Wyndham meeting they would find out what the class of 77 was willing to do to stay alive.

Claudette's cousins were still pouring in the next day, from Memphis her cousin Priscilla and her teenage girls, J'nyla and J'Leeah and her dad Donnie.

Tracy came in with a team of truck drivers and the letters she had pilfered out of the mail. There were two people who lived not too far in Fairview. They had a plan to go to their homes and hold them there and find substitutes with a likeness to the hostages that would attend the clandestine meeting and record every word.

Tomorrow we will have a meeting at the Wyndham, by then everyone will be here, and we can brainstorm. Around midnight everyone who needed to go to the hotel left for the night and would return in the morning. Some left their children since they were all playing so well together. There were tents set up in the backyard with cots.

CHAPTER 13
FROM A CHILD'S EYES
CHAVONNE AND
DAVID

Most of the children were under the impression that they were on vacation. The next morning Malcolm spoke to all the parents when they arrived. "Your children are not stupid. They know that something is happening and even though this is something that you would like to hide from them for their own protection they should be educated about what we are dealing with. Does anyone have a problem with me having someone talk to them."

The few who disagreed changed their view when they were told, "How can your children protect themselves if they are oblivious to the fact, they are prey. We need to flip the script on the enemy and train the kids to defend themselves. You will also need to go through the same training.

Malcolm asked Claudette if he could have Chavonne and Lloyd

Jr. talk to the kids and explain things to them from a child's point of view before the grown-ups start giving them directions.

"Sure"

"Chavonne and David can I speak with you for a moment?"

They were outside in a circle playing a game of Disney charades. They rose and followed him into Darrien's office. "I need the two of you to show the kids the videos and tell them what is going down. Can you handle that? Malcolm asked.

"Yes," Chavonne said.

"Sure," David said.

When they got outside, they called all the kids together. Malcolm stood behind them.

"We want to tell you guys why you are here. We don't want you to get scared, we have all got to be really brave. You understand?" David said.

They all nodded their heads.

"Have you guys seen the movie Independence Day with Will Smith?" David said.

Most of them had seen the movie and started talking about it. What had happened in it, "Will Smith whooped them Aliens asses." J'Nyla spoke.

"There are aliens and government people who want to kill us and our parents, they are going to set off a satellite that is going to blow everything up, you guys saw on the news all those people who are being killed in Compton?" Chavonne said.

"My momma said that all her friends that she went to school with are getting killed." Shaquita, Wandas granddaughter said.

The parents were encouraged to attend the meeting so they would be able to explain any questions their children had. Priscilla sat between her two girls because she really did not understand what was happening herself.

"That's because someone in their class found out about their plans and told some people at the class reunion. Since they don't know who she told they are just trying to kill everyone in the class of 1977." Chavonne said.

"We are going to teach you guys how to fight and shoot, because you are going to need to protect yourselves and your friends and family. Are you all down with that?" Malcolm asked.

"Man, I will blow them aliens up, give me a AK47 and I will blast them fools." Lil Hakim said.

Many of the kids were excited as they talked about what they would do to the aliens. After they quieted down a bit, Malcolm continued "We are going to need all you shorty's to be brave and always be careful, we are going to teach you guys everything you need to know to be soldiers.

The kids were ready, they could not wait to kill something. The video game generation was ready for anything, and they could use that to their advantage. They were planning to use the drones to wipe out every alien that Gordon had a list of. The kids could do that from a computer at headquarters with the help of the satellite cameras they were going to hack into. Alex would design a program that gave a target, and the mission was to annihilate that target. To the kids it would be playing a video game, when in actuality they would be killing aliens and key government personnel.

"Did I do alright?" David asked.

"Fo Sho Little man, hey how many video games you got with shooting and driving? "

"I got a Sega, Xbox and a Dreamcast. Why?"

Because I have a mission for you. I want you to get these kids practicing some games. How many T.V.'s you guys have to use?"

"Four"

"That's not enough. Tell you what, I'm going to get Adam to take you and two others, you pick out who. You get ten T.V. sets, some x-boxes, GameCube, PlayStation, whatever you think is the best along with everything you need to go with it, games, controllers, the whole nine yards. Can you do that?"

"Yo, are you serious? I know all the good games. Me and my big brother will get all the hook ups."

Lloyd Jr. ran off to get Davonne. They found Adam and were off in no time. James went along, he was instructed to get targets and B.B. guns. Later they would take everyone to a paintball range that Chavonne had told him about. They would all learn how to aim, of course shooting real guns was a little bit different, but paintball was a way to start.

Everyone was eating breakfast, that the women had prepared. Pancakes, sausage fruit cups and bacon were on the tables along with orange juice, milk and cereal. Everyone had ideas that they were writing down so that they could coordinate at the next meeting.

Claudette's family had arrived, all of them were ready to do whatever it took.

Eugene and his chapter of the Black Underground were coordinating everyone who could work on the Sportsplex, those who did not know how to do construction were assigned to work with someone who did, before long they would pick up the mechanics of the job. They would also get some how to books and videos that they could study. They had carpenters who would work on a team headed by her uncle Curly. He had a construction company in California building houses for over thirty years. A back injury would not allow him to be hands on, but he could train anyone.

Jim Dale had called a neighborhood association emergency meeting, and they all met at his home. He played the videotapes that he had borrowed from Gordon, and they all sat in horror at what they knew could be them at any moment. They were all willing to help and offered space in their homes to house people until they could get more permanent housing. There were engineers, electricians and plumbers, they all did work around their homes so they would make perfect candidates for the sportsplex project.

CHAPTER 14
THINNING THE
POPULATION

Two aliens were meeting about ways to thin the populace.

"Tsumani bombs strategically placed on the ocean floor will wipe out all the Islands. "

"Hurricanes can wipe out the beach states."

"Earthquakes and tornadoes are good for the interior cities."

"Well, we have already flooded the markets with ephedrine, and before that we had Phen Phen, we took out a few hundred thousand. What gets me is that these people see the tort attorneys on the news advertising that this weight loss medicine is killing people but rather than take the fork out of their mouths, push their obese asses away from the table, get up take a walk, or go to the gym, they all want to take the secret, magic pill."

"Or they want to go and get carved up like a thanksgiving turkey."

"How about the lypo-suction where they get their asses and thighs vacuumed?"

"When the fat comes back it can't go to the same place, so it has to find other places to settle."

"Like the side of their neck or the back of an armpit."

"We got rid of a lot of them with the boob implants in the 70's. I have come up with an improved source of poison that we can put in the new saline implants. Within two years the poison leaks into their system, they are left with deflated bags, much like flat tires on a car. The silicone bag bonds with their tissue and melts into their system, within four months they expire, that should be good for at least two million deaths."

"It is as if everyone is walking around with implants. They give them out with puberty now. Have you seen those models? They are no more than children that they have plumped up to get them on magazine covers."

"Tits and ass sell in this country."

"Do not get me started on asses, what about the ones who put industrial silicon from Home Depot in their asses until it turns black because not enough oxygen is getting to it.

"If I could find one with a real set of Double D's who isn't built like a bus, I would make sure that she gets into the shelter."

"Good luck with that, it would be like finding a needle in a haystack."

"That's what I need a big needle, I could go around pricking each one until I find one that doesn't deflate or spring a leak," They laughed.

"I have an idea, how about we enhance the sex enhancement drugs. You know Viagra, Vigel, Cialis."

"What did you have in mind?"

"Their pecker doesn't stop growing and explodes."

"How about as soon as they ejaculate all their plasma goes out with the semen, like a super orgasm."

"They come and they go," he broke out into raucous laughter about his own joke.

"We are wiping out a lot of men with prostrate and colon cancer."

"Works extremely well with the African Americans."

"Well in all my clinics, I am having sudden deaths, caused by reactions to anesthesia. We are having thousands of nicked bowels, which causes irritable bowel syndrome and adhesions. It entails several surgeries because every time you touch the bowel you must go in and clear the adhesion, which will require another surgery six months later like a merry go round. Now we have produced a wonder drug, which will eventually cause the bowel to dissolve, leaking feces into their systems. They will feel as if their symptoms have been alleviated but when it starts to dissolve the organs it works within twenty-four hours, not enough time for doctors to stop it. There is nothing left for the autopsy either, this is going to baffle the shit out of them, literally."

"The next thing is the senior citizens; we are going through the medicines that are most popular with them. We have a drug that will cure arthritis but within a year the liver fails.

"As a psychiatrist I am going to start prescribing more ativan, paxil, Prozac, all the serotonin-inhibitors. That should take care of half the population because no one is comfortable in their own skin."

"We also must start taping into the Ritalin that these mothers are giving their kids, I would never let my children go on that stuff, it inhibits their natural spirit. If a kid is acting up you physically chastise them, do not drug them into little zombies."

"We only have a few more years before D-day."

"The humans do not realize that the water that keeps them alive is killing them. They have come up with a process that desalinates and purifies sewage water. The feces are all poison that the body doesn't need and eliminates. They cannot get all the medicines and diseases out, which means they are hydrating themselves to death."

"Cancer and other diseases are the results of their tainted water. No matter how much they filter, they are poisoning themselves one glass at a time. Their bodies are made up of mostly fluids, so they have no choice but to drink."

"Their food sources are contaminated from water, pesticides and the growth hormones. The clouds take the evaporated ocean water over the land, and it waters the crops and the livestock eats the grass and plant life that is no better than their purified water which results in obesity, high blood pressure and cholesterol issues."

"We are enhancing the recreational drugs. The stronger we make them the more dependent the addicts get."

"They are homeless zombies with nothing more on their minds

than their next fix. Between the prescriptions and the methamphetamine, heroin, cocaine which we have added fentanyl to make the veins close and disintegrate, they are going to be dead within months. You would think that the corpses that are popping up all over the place would deter them, but it does not, they have weak minds controlled by drugs."

"They have developed meds that take away the addicts' cravings, the insurance companies would rather pay to keep these products off the market."

"I think we have come up with a good outline, we have more than enough notes to keep us busy for the next year. I am going to knock off for the day."

Two minutes after they left the office a janitor walked into the room and started cleaning. When he was sure no one was around he climbed onto the table and took the tape that was in the hidden camera behind the light fixture.

CHAPTER 15
BERNARD

B ernard Sheiderman had been in love with Sally Spei-
gal since Jr. High School, she was the star of every wet
dream he ever had. She had been the homecoming queen,
a cheerleader, the president of the modeling club. Of course, he being the
geeky nerd that he was, she had never noticed him, except for one time
when he gave the winning answer at the state spelling bee and brought
the trophy home for the school, she had ran up to him and hugged him
saying "good job," before she disappeared into the crowd. The way she
felt pressed up against him, the intoxicating smell of her hair, he re-
played that moment in his mind for years.

He had never forgotten her, all his years at MIT, he compared
every girl he dated to her, and they never measured up.

When he went home to Cambridge to visit his family, his gay
cousin, Georgie always brought him up to speed on the small-town gos-

sip.

Georgie lived right next door to Sally and her ex-Jock husband, Larry, who was physically abusing her. Once when he went home, she had just suffered a miscarriage, the result of a beating. She and Georgie were best friends, and he had tried dozens of times to get her to leave the brut, but she was afraid.

Sally was not allowed to go anywhere without Larry, he even accompanied her to the grocery store. If she went anywhere on her own, he would fly into an abusive rage and accuse her of all kinds of things that she would never do.

What a difference fifteen years can make. Yes, the tables had turned. Larry, the star MVP football player, who was Sally's boyfriend in school, was now a grease monkey at a gas station in Jersey. Sally had made the mistake of marrying him right after graduation, he was destined to be a professional ball player, but an injury left him with no hope of ever living out that dream. His first year playing college ball, Larry had been mowed down causing irreparable damage to his knee, he was left with a limp and did not have the brains to make it scholastically.

He never went back to college. He worked in his Uncle Vince's garage. He took his bitterness and disappointment out on his wife every Friday night, when he got drunk on what was left of his paycheck.

His uncle held out enough money to pay Larry's bills and give Sally an allowance. He owned the house that they rented. Thankfully, utilities were included, or Sally would have had to live in the dark with no water.

Vince had raised Larry after his father had been drunk enough to run into a light pole and the car blew up. Vince recognized the signs of the disease in his nephew. He knew what an alcoholic did with money, he drank it. along with their wives, home homes and jobs.

Vince had just received his twenty-year chip from Alcoholics Anonymous. He had beaten two wives into divorce court. The third wife would only agree to marry him if he sobered up. She was the best thing that had ever happened to him. She was his brother's widow, and Larry's mother.

Vince had raised him since the age of ten and had been proud of the boy. He was on the right track with football, but the death of his father and the death of his career, followed by his mother's demise from cancer, was just too much disappointment for him to bear.

Larry tried going to AA meetings with his uncle, but it only made him want to have a drink. He only agreed to go after he had beaten Sally. The next day he always felt repentant, and promised he would stop drinking. It never lasted and for ten years he had been beating her looks and spirit away. He had peaked early in life and fizzled out like a sparkler on the fourth of July.

Meanwhile Bernard had gone on to college for almost ten years, upon his graduation he had five companies bidding to hire him. His first year in pharma he developed a cure for Parkinson's disease. After that he could write his own ticket. Pharmaceutical companies begged to fund his research.

Bernards shelves and walls featured his medical science awards, including a Nobel Peace Prize. He had been on the cover of dozens of magazines which made him somewhat of a celebrity. He was one of the richest and most eligible bachelors on the planet. He dated a lot because he was expected to walk in with someone on his arm to the many functions he had to attend. He never went out with the same woman twice.

He had just gone through a paternity case, when a scorned European model named him the father of her child. The case had been well publicized on Court TV. A Q-tip had proven him not to be the father. He had more money than he knew what to do with, but no one to do it with.

When Bernard heard that Sally was in the hospital with a broken jaw and a concussion, and to top it off had suffered a miscarriage, he went with Georgie to visit her.

"Why would you even consider going back to that monster. Don't you realize that he is going to kill you one day? He just murdered your child for Christ's sake wake up, you can do better. You are not some punching bag for a washed-up jock," Georgie asked.

"I have nowhere else to go. I didn't go to college, I have no skills, my parents are dead, I have no family, I don't have a choice," Sally cried.

"Yes, you do," Bernard said.

"What do you mean?" she asked.

"I mean that you can come and live with me in New York until you get on your feet. Don't worry about a job, you can work for me."

"Doing what?"

"I just bought a mansion in Long Island. I work long hours and sometimes my work takes me away for weeks at a time, you could take care of decorating the place and housesit. I'll pay you, and if you want to go to school, I will pay for that too."

"That is perfect, and Larry would not have a clue as to where you are. Bernie, this is a splendid idea, she can cook for you, she is pretty good in the kitchen. It will put an end to all that nuked food you eat, which you know is not healthy," Georgie said.

"What about my things? I get out of here tomorrow at noon, Larry does not know. I could not impose on you Bernard, it's a sweet offer but I would like I was taking advantage of you."

"I must hire someone, why not you? The house has three floors, so there will be more than enough to keep you busy. You will have carte blanche. We will find you a decorator to work with. I just got the keys last month and I do not have time to buy a bed, let alone a house full of furniture. Come on, it will be fun, when is the last time you decorated a mansion?"

"Girl, you cannot go back to that man, this is your chance to get away, Cinderella. Go for it," Georgie said.

The next morning when Larry left for work, Georgie and Bernard crept into Sally's house and packed everything on the list she had given them. When Bernard looked at her tattered clothes that were no more than outdated, secondhand rags, he told Georgie "Leave the clothes, I will give you two some money and you can go shopping when we get to New York."

"What do you mean, We?"

"Aren't you tired of being in this town year in and year out, besides you can help Sally with the transition, what better person to help polish her into my trophy wife."

"Boy, are you moving fast, you want to marry her?"

"First I have to dazzle her with my charms."

"And your money, I think that she would make you a wonderful wife, and she would be away from that abusive bastard, Larry. I think that with a gentle hand it is just a matter of time before she will be yours. You know she sits around in those four rooms reading romance novels because he never takes her anywhere. You could take her to some plays, the ballet, shopping in Manhattan, some clubs, she hasn't been out of Cambridge since she married Larry."

"See, that is exactly why I need your help. You are her best friend in the world. You could coach me on what she likes and what I should do to get her to marry me. Georgie, I have been in love with her for more than fifteen years. Will you come?"

New York was wonderful for Sally. As soon as she could get up and move around, she and Georgie went shopping in all the designer stores Manhattan had to offer, Gucci, Donna Karan, and Versace, she could not get enough of the stores. One day, as they lunched at Wolfgang Pucks, she was comparing herself to these gorgeous women in the upscale restaurant. "They all have the perfect little pert nose, and their breasts look as if they were sculpted, maybe I should get a nose job," she confided to Georgie.

"That's a good idea, because it hasn't healed properly after the dozens of times Larry broke it. While you are at it, why not get some tits too, maybe even some butt implants, you could have one of those J-Lo booties. You know Bernie is an ass man."

"Why would you say that? Bernard is not interested in me that way."

"Girl, Larry must have hit you in the head one too many times, Bernard is in love with you and has been since Jr. High. Duh, Honey, he is your knight in shining armor."

"You think he likes me? He is never even around."

"That's because he is working on some big thingamajig in Dallas, he is one of the most renowned scientists in the world. Trust me, honey, he didn't bring you out here for nothing. You had better get with the program girl, you could be the first Mrs. Bernard Sheiderman and do not think that there aren't plenty of women after him. He has to beat them off with sticks. Actors, supermodels you name it, he has had them. You want to know why he has never gotten serious with anyone because he compares them all to you. That's why he never married; I know he may not look like much, but he is beautiful."

"I find Bernard incredibly attractive, besides, I have been with the pretty boy jock and look what it got me. I cannot compete with supermodels and actors."

"Oh yes you can, we are going to get you into etiquette classes, I hate to say it honey but you have the table manners of a horse. We are going to take you to the best plastic surgeon in town. We could get our noses done on the buddy plan. A good hairdresser and you can compete with the best of them. Bernard will be back in a couple of days, then he leaves for a month, which is when we will schedule your surgery, when he comes back you have undergone a total transformation. Are you game?"

"Do you think that I could one day be Mrs. Sheiderman," she

said with a twinkle in her eye.

"Honey if I can't get you and Bernie engaged within the year, I will go straight."

"That will never happen," she laughed.

"You just leave it to Georgie."

He took out a cell phone and made some calls, by the time they finished lunch he had bribed a secretary to put them down for a consultation that afternoon. A week later they both underwent surgery. They had to pay a little extra to get appointments so soon after the consultation. George had rhinoplasty. Sally had rhinoplasty, breast implants and a lift, and butt implants, not much just enough to take out the gravity droop.

Georgie took care of her; he cooked and gave her sponge baths. He messaged her so that her implants would not get hard. As they recuperated, they had interior decorators coming and going to the Manhattan penthouse. They ordered beds and as soon as they were in, they moved to the house in Long Island to supervise all the deliveries. Georgie taught her how to surf the net, soon she was cybershopping with the best of them. She bought all kinds of furniture, dishes, clothes, and art. She also tuned into the shopping channels. She had two platinum credit cards and boy was she using them.

Georgie hired a landscape architect who was appalled when he said that he wanted a vegetable garden close to the house, he persuaded him to erect a greenhouse farther back to avoid having pesky animals and ants invading the pool area.

Georgie decided to have a barn erected and hired someone to help him purchase horses. The same guy would take care of them every day and teach Georgie and Sally how to ride.

Sally and the mansion were transformed. When Bernard came back from his trip that had kept him away for a month, he could not believe how nice the house looked.

When Bernard saw Sally come down the stairs in an Armani

gown, his heart skipped a beat. She had prepared a candlelight dinner. After dinner, she showed him around the newly decorated house, complete with a lab that boasted all the newest technology, as he requested. Finally, they had gone through all forty rooms. The tour ended in her bedroom. The fireplace was lit, and the flames reflected off the peach-canopied bed. He went into the bathroom to relieve himself.

When he walked back into the bedroom, she lay naked on the satin comforter. He could not get out of his clothes fast enough. He took his time exploring and tasting every crevice of her body. She had never had an orgasm with Larry. She could not believe how her body was responding to his touch. Even the vibrator she used every day when Larry went to work had not made her feel this way. She rode wave after wave of ecstasy.

For Bernard, this was the reality of the fantasies that he lived with every night. No woman had ever brought him to these heights. No woman tasted so good, like candy and when he felt the little bundle of nerves throb under his tongue and heard her moans that sounded like little whimpers, it urged him on. When he finally could not take it anymore and lifted himself to enter her she slid down and took his turgid phallus into her mouth, he felt like he was being engulfed in warm velvet, he could not stop himself, he exploded and she took every ounce of his juices. He tried to move away but she gripped him tighter and continued to suck and lick until he became hard again. She pushed him down and mounted him. She rode him as if she were on a horse, positioning herself so that her swollen clitoris could hit every nerve until she collapsed on top of him. He got up and pulled her up onto her knees entering her from behind and moved in hard piston-like thrust that turned her whimpers to screams. He yelled so loud when he came that the sound echoed through the entire house. They snuggled under the covers and bathed in the afterglow of good sex.

They heard footsteps running up the stairs, Georgie burst into the room holding a golf club, he had heard what sounded like a wounded animal from the other side of the house and thought maybe there was a burglar. They laughed as they looked at the expression on his face change from protector to embarrassment when he realized what was going on.

"Oh my god, you guys were up here doing the do. I thought someone was getting killed or that some wild animal was in the house, O.K. kids give up the goods, how was it? I want details, start talking," Georgie said.

Within six months Bernard and Sally were engaged.

Bernard arranged for a lawyer to pay Larry fifty thousand dollars to sign divorce papers. As expected, he haggled until he got one hundred thousand, he had seen Sally on the cover of that hoity-toity magazine 'House Beautiful.' They were always in the tabloids. He could not wait to get his hands on one hundred thousand dollars. The lawyer had been told that he could go as high as three hundred thousand.

Their relationship was a fairytale, they traveled and not a night went by that they did not make love. She went with him to Dallas when he was going to be there for more than two days, he did not want to be without her. They bought a condo in the Turtle Creek area of Dallas. They went to France, and she fell in love with the countryside. He bought her a chateau.

Two years to the day that Bernard had taken Sally from the hospital to her new life, they married in New York, while four hundred people looked on.

CHAPTER 16
GEORGIE

G eorgie had undergone a physical exam before having rhinoplasty. A few weeks later when he went back for a postoperative appointment he had been given some disturbing news. He had AIDS.

When he and Sally rode in the limousine back home he told her. She held him as he cried. When they got home, she called Bernard in Dallas. "Bernard, I have some bad news, Georgie has AIDS, we just came from the doctor, and they told him, what can we do?"

"I'm going to arrange a plane for the two of you. Be at the airport in two hours."

"What are you going to do?"

"I know of a procedure that has worked on several AIDS victims. Trust me, honey, I can fix this, get moving, I will have a car waiting to bring you to the Lab from the airport, I will meet you there.

Bernard hung up the phone and went into one of his colleague's offices. Morty was in his natural alien form. "I need your help."

"O.K. have a seat."

"My cousin has AIDS; I want to cure him, and I know that you have helped several people with the disease."

"Well, you know that the only people that we have done this costly procedure on are scheduled to go into the shelter. Is your cousin on that list?"

Bernard realized that there was no way Georgie could meet the criteria. He had been sickly as a child and he was gay - a definite disqualifier. "Yes, he is. He works with the CDC and contracted the disease from a needle that a patient pulled out of himself and stabbed him with. He is a brilliant scientist," Bernard said as he handed Mork a dummied-up folder with forged documents.

"I don't need that; your word is good enough for me. When would you like to do the procedure, you know that he will have to stay here and be monitored for a few weeks." Mork said.

"He will be here in a few hours; I would like to prep him and get underway first thing in the morning if possible."

"O.K. we need his blood type, for the transfusion. The procedure has been quite successful, we pull out several pints of blood a day and give him medicines that work much like antibiotics, at the same time we pump in healthy blood treated with chemicals designed to attack any weak cells. We have a ninety percent success rate. I will see you in the morning."

Bernard picked up the folder and walked out of the room to make the necessary arrangements.

Mork knew that his head scientist was lying. He knew everything there was to know about Bernard Sheiderman and every other person who worked in this lab. He knew about George, who cruised gay bars in Greenwich Village picking up sexual partners, he also knew that he was no more a scientist than the sky was green. George and Bernard's wife Sally had undergone some cosmetic surgery recently. It was done at one of their clinics. He had been alerted as soon as they called. He had told them to make sure that they did not have any problems, rather than the faulty silicone implants Larry had coerced her to get, they swapped them out for saltwater.

Nothing was added to their anesthesia, which was what they did to make people sick and in a couple of years expire.

Mork knew that he needed Bernard, he was a wonderful scientist in the areas of medical science, geneticist, chemicals, horticulture, and marine life. He was imperative to the success of the mission and would be a great help when they went into the shelter. He would do the procedure for George, no matter how much he detested homosexuals, he knew that Georgie was Bernard's closest relative, next to his parents and his wife. He could always be eliminated later.

Mork called his assistant in to discuss this. "We know that Bernard has lied, it is a human weakness, he cares for his cousin and wants to save him, even though his lifestyle would be detrimental to the mission. We will do the procedure and after we are in the shelter, we will eliminate George."

They rose to leave for the day, when they had left the floor, a janitor entered the office and took a wire from behind a picture, the recorder was in a closet, he took out the tape, finished cleaning the office, and left for the day.

Sally and Georgie had just deplaned and boarded a helicopter to the office, when they arrived on the roof of the company, nurses took Georgie away for preliminary testing. He lay in a hospital bed.

"What does Bernie think he is up to?" Georgie asked.

"He is going to help you, have some faith." Sally said.

"Honey, there is no cure for AIDS."

"You don't know that. God can cure anything, how did you become gay anyway?"

"Chile, you don't become gay you are born that way, I knew in Jr. high school that I liked looking at the boys more than I did the girls. You know this is the first time I have ever regretted my lifestyle."

"Don't worry, Bernie is going to help, he can fix anything."

"Chile, you think that Bernie is God or something, he didn't create the world in seven days you know, or say let there be light, he is just a man."

"Well, I wouldn't say all that, he may be just a man, but he is about to be a father too."

"Really girl," Georgie hugged her. "I am so happy for you, if anyone deserves to be happy it is you and Bernie. I just hope I'm around long enough to see the little crumb snatcher grow up."

"You have to, you are going to be the Godparent."

"Be serious, I am not exactly what you might call a good role model."

"You are to me, and Bernie, and I know that you would be a wonderful guardian."

"I haven't told him yet, so don't say anything. O.K."

"Sure."

Bernie came into the room, "Look we have had great success with this procedure, I want you to get some rest, and I will see you bright and early."

After they left George sat looking into the dark and his past. He never found a solid relationship, thus the necessity to prowl the gay establishments. He had a long list of one-nighters. Maybe when they did the transfusion the desire to be gay would get chased out.

He envied Bernard and Sally, the promise of a life together waking up with someone every day, and the children they would have. If this went well, he swore to do something about his promiscuous ways. At least he would protect himself with condoms and maybe find a steady. It would be great if when they did the transfusion the desire to be gay would leave his body, but for that to happen he would need a lobotomy.

He envied Bernard and Sally, the promise of a life together, and waking up with someone by your side every day. He never imagined having children of his own. He once brought up the subject with his sister, Nan, about the possibility of her being a surrogate for him. He immediately regretted bringing up the topic with her. She was ranting so loud his other sisters came into the room and they all went full force preaching about him being an abomination and that God did not create men to sleep together, but to procreate to have children and create families, which two guys cannot do. The bottom line was they did not think children should be raised by anything but a female mother and male father, preferably married.

If this procedure went well, he swore to do something about his promiscuous ways and think about going straight. At the very least he would protect himself with condoms and attempt to find a steady, at least long enough to have some children. Or he could consider hiring a surrogate to carry his seed. But being a single parent would be a challenge. He would discuss the topic with Sally, he knew that she would step up and help.

The nurse breezed in and put something in his IV that made him sleep.

CHAPTER 17
BERNARD

B ernard lay in bed watching Sally as she slept. She was in the habit of kicking off her covers in her sleep. He studied her nudity from the Texas morning sun that bathed and illuminated every gorgeous crease and bend. Her breasts seemed to have gotten larger. He knew she had been augmented, but this was something different. They had a lushness about them, and the areolas were wider. His gaze traveled down to her stomach, there was a slight paunch, kind of like what it would look like if she had ingested a huge meal. "Oh My god!" he said aloud and dared to hope. Could it be? He reached out and touched her stomach, her eyes fluttered open. She saw the question in his eyes. She opened the bedside drawer and took out an E.P.T. test stick. She held it up so that he could see the pink + plus sign that confirmed he was going to be a father. "So, what do you have to say - daddy?"

Bernard had never cried in front of anyone before, even when his grandfather died, he could not cry until he was alone. He did not realize that tears were falling down his face. "A child, I am going to have a child. You know I never even knew that I wanted one until this very moment."

"So, I guess that this is alright with you?"

"It's more than alright," He sat up and gathered her into his arms.

"I've never seen you cry before."

"What do you mean?"

She reached up and wiped a tear from his cheek onto her finger. He looked at it and then put his hand to his face and felt the water. "I didn't realize I was crying, I guess I'm just so happy."

They fell asleep, her back to him and his arms around her stomach.

Bernard woke to the sound of the doorbell. He rose and made his way to the door and signed the package. He disappeared into his lab. He opened the box and removed the video. The private investigator had edited out anything he did not think Bernard needed to be worried about. It started with a recording of Mork and his plans to kill Georgie after they entered the shelter.

Bernard's career was built around finding drugs to reverse physical maladies, and here the aliens were discussing how they were going to distort his life's work to kill people. He watched the tape about them wiping the planet clean. He had not had a clue that they were planning global extinction. It was a senseless stupid thing to do, and he was not going to be a part of it. He picked up the phone. Per the directions that came in the box, he phoned Alex Hamilton and made plans to dine with their wives that night.

That evening Alex Hamilton and Malcolm brought Bernard up to speed on everything. He knew about the sportsplex, which when he took the job had been told that it would double as a shelter. He had helped with the design of the emergency shelter. One of his projects was to work on food and sustenance.

Bernard developed a program that could read genealogical signatures through a simple blood test. Since it was something that the public could buy, there was a rash of men finding out that the children they had been raising were not theirs. Not only men, in one demographic area they had found out that several children had been swapped around in the delivery room. Someone had a twisted sense of humor. After they investigated and narrowed down the culprit to a drug-addicted nurse who had lost her license and was incarcerated. There was a social media club of the parents who had given birth during her term of employment at hospitals throughout her career, and Bernard's program helped these parents to identify and locate their true children.

The club had also used the program when it was discovered that a doctor was substituting his super sperm in women who were undergoing IVF, Invitro fertilization treatments. He manipulated his sperm through science into a super potent, sure-shot version. and they found he had fathered over three thousand redheaded children which resulted in another social media club.

Bernard's super food grower would feed the chosen few who entered the shelter. Meanwhile, he had started organizations that went around to impoverished communities and churches to create community gardens that would help people have the God-given right to eat. They purchased land in the neighborhoods and supplied everything they needed to get started, including fruit trees, herbs, vegetables, and berries. People came in to help them bring their gardens to fruition.

Bernard's life-saving work in medicine would be a threat to pharma companies by the time he was done. They would not be lining their pockets and living their opulent lives on his hard work because he stepped in to ensure the price would be affordable to the people who needed it. Pharma did not like his terms, but the alternative would be losing him to the competition, a reality he made clear at every meeting before taking his leave. He stood outside the conference room doors and mumbled his mantra, "Oh I have my work cut out for me, but I am going to make a better world."

At the meeting with Alex Hamilton who had invited Malcolm and his significant other. Malcolm had been in the closet for decades about his sexuality, but in light of the current events he decided not to worry about anyone else's opinion and was going to be true to himself from now on. Anybody who didn't like it should have a look at his record and the thousands of kills he had racked up in numerous wars before they opened their mouths.

Alex had also invited Sharilyn and Gordon who queried, "There will be a big meeting at the Wyndham Hotel tomorrow. We have people working in all phases of the shelter. Can we count on your help?"

Before Bernard could answer Malcolm interrupted, "May I ask why you are vested in this endeavor?"

Bernard said, "I recently found out what the sportsplex was about. I was told that the sportsplex would double as an emergency long-term shelter and I did a lot of development on various parts of the planning process, food, sleeping quarters, marine life reproduction; you name it somewhere in every section of that building you will find my name on the designs."

"That in itself makes you invaluable to what we are trying to accomplish," Gordon said.

"My life's work has been to help eradicate diseases and manage maladies like arthritis, aids, cancer, and Parkinson's, not to mention a few thousand problems that we were able to avert with an injection that stopped the problem from turning into a full-blown pandemic, so people can enjoy life. To answer your question, I recently hired a private investigator to do some digging for me and when I discovered that one of my medicines was resulting in deaths through security footage, I found out that they had distorted my recipe for a drug that was losing them money because people were cured of arthritis."

"You are talking about Arthcure. I just lost my uncle behind that mess. And countless military men have died," Sharilyn said.

"The change they made resulted in millions of deaths, on that same footage I found that someone very close to me who 'how shall I put this,' plays on your team,' has Aids. I worked with them to develop a cure. As we speak, he is undergoing the procedure, but the fact that he is gay makes him ineligible for the shelter, so I lied about his lifestyle and occupation to get him help," Bernard said.

"We have a lot of friends who could benefit from that procedure, why does the public not know about this? Sherry, Malcolm's transvestite life partner asked.

"On the same footage, I discovered that they already knew everything there was to know about my cousin, he should not have even been given the cure because of his homosexuality, but they did it to appease me. They plan to dispose of him later after he is allowed into the shelter. Those are my reasons. I know I can be a tremendous asset to your organization."

"Hell yeah, that's what I'm talking about," Alex looked at Malcolm. "Any more reservations?"

"Nope, not a one, welcome to the Black Underground," Malcolm shook Bernard's hand.

"But I am not black," Bernard said.

We don't care," Gordon said.

"This calls for a celebration," Alex gestured for the waiter and ordered two bottles of champagne."

CHAPTER 18
THE MEETING

P eople had come from everywhere, relatives and friends
had been alerted and though it took some convincing,
they were present. They had taken every room in the
local hotels, and many were staying as guests of Darrien's neighbors.
Twenty homes had been purchased in the surrounding vicinity.

Alex, Malcolm, Bernard, Gordon, and Franklin headed to the
meeting. They went into detail about the plan they had put together.
Gordon had a list of the undercover aliens, and they were eliminating
the key players first to cut down on the opposition.

They assigned people to do different tasks, like maids' jani-
tors, and gardeners to infiltrate the alien's homes and workplaces. They
would not start killing them until a week before D-day. Each death
would appear to be an accident so no one could put two and two together. Franklin worked out where to employ as many people as he possibly

could, taking advantage of their skills and training. They would build the shelter to spec but with a few undetectable changes that would allow them access to the building when the time came.

They had been informed by the marines that the murders were drawing too much media attention. They were ordered to stand down. Since they were the team assigned to the murders they would be given task at a later date. This window would be a good time for the alumni to go back and sell their homes and monetize anything they could. They needed to buy gold as currency was not going to be of any value.

When they returned, they would board the planes under their new identities, that way they would not be tracked back to Texas. At that time the marines would stage their deaths. Headquarters would monitor the movements of the Aliens and the Government officials that they knew were involved.

Bernard was working on a way to identify the Aliens from humans. They could not come up with a way to stop the detonation that was scheduled to go off in approximately six months.

Bernard sat in the dark living room with a glass of Raynal in his hand. The excitement about the baby had waned. He realized that if the Government had its way, he would never see his child born. He had watched tapes of them planning not only to kill Georgie but Sally also, her family had too many illnesses that could be passed on genetically, even if she did not get the cancer or the leukemia that had killed her parents, their child surely would. Now he knew why millions were left to die and only a few were being saved with the cures they were hoarding.

Bernard hated the thought of losing Sally and the baby, which he really would have done had he not been contacted by the Black Underground. "I am going to give them damn aliens a taste of their own medicine," he said aloud as tears fell from his eyes. He did not realize that Sally was in the room until the light came on, and by then it was too late for him to hide his tears.

Sally sat on his lap, she had never seen him cry she had never seen any man cry, other than Georgie. She touched his face with the back of his hand. The contact brought forth a flood of emotions, he hid his face on her shoulder and started sobbing.

Sally did not question Bernard, whatever was wrong he would tell her in his own time. She was afraid that it must be something terrible. He was always so calm and always had it together, it was a little unnerving to see him like this.

Georgie was returning from one of his midnight excursions into town where he hung around an adult bookstore until he met someone. He used two condoms instead of one. He was fortunate enough to have beaten HIV once, he was not going to tempt fate. He was angry with himself and depressed as he always was afterward to not have been able to keep the vows that he made when he was close to losing his life.

Aside from the two seconds it took him to ejaculate it had been a very unsatisfying encounter. The guy he picked up was nice enough, and he felt guilty when he gave him a false name and phone number. He had never wanted to be in a relationship, he just wanted to get his satisfaction and go home and forget it ever happened.

He knew he was gay, but he did not want to share his life with a gay man, one pathetic person in a house was enough.

Georgie wondered why the light in the living room was on at three in the morning. He found Sally sitting on Bernard's lap sleeping.

"Sally, Bernie what are you two doing sleeping in here?"

Bernard opened his swollen eyes. "We must have fallen asleep."

"I came down and found Bernard here, drinking and crying," Sally said.

"What's going on Bernie?"

"I have to show you two something, go into the den and I will be right there, I have to get something out of the car."

Georgie helped Sally out of the seat, she went into the kitchen and fixed herself a peanut butter and pickle sandwich, she had an affinity for the strangest foods lately. She picked up her tray with strawberry milk, Cheetos, jellybeans and her sandwich and walked into the den. Bernard was putting in a videotape tape and the huge screen was dropping down from the ceiling taking up the whole wall.

The Sony projector showed a board room, and some men dressed in costumes that looked like they were on the cast of Star Trek, along with men in military uniforms. "Why are we watching a sci-fi movie at this time of the morning?" Georgie asked.

"Please, pay attention, this is very important," Bernard said as he turned up the volume.

"How are we going to handle Bernard's family? We need him. He is a brilliant scientist and an important key to the success of our mission."

"Well, we can't have that homosexual running around in the shelter. The last reports have him out skulking around adult bookstores looking for sexual partners. Can you believe it, we just completed the operation that saved him from a debilitating disease, and he is out there campaigning for another dose. We informed him that the procedure could not be repeated. We have no choice but to eliminate him."

"Sally's genetic history indicates that she is a prime candidate for several diseases, mind you she may not get sick, but the child is almost certain to come up with something. She also has a history of miscarriage, even if she was able to reproduce there is no guarantee she will carry to term, and though we can cure her, the children would be high risk, I say we eliminate her also. We can make it a car accident with the two of them."

"I think that it should be separate incidents. I would love to see that fag fall on his own sword; we could make it look as if another homosexual killed him."

"How do you think that the loss will affect Bernard? You know these humans can become withdrawn and have mental problems."

"That's just a chance we will have to take. We can eliminate them after we get them into the shelter, Bernard will be told that it is a six-month experiment. He does not have to know the true mission until it is too late for him to do anything to complicate matters, I do believe that there is a boy scout deep inside of Bernard."

Bernard turned off the television,

"Were they talking about me?" Sally asked with wide eyes.

"What is this shit, Bernard?" Georgie shouted.

He took a long time explaining about the aliens who had been here for hundreds of years, he explained the government's role. Finally, he told him about the shelter.

"The Black Underground, along with Alex Hamilton, discovered the conspiracy. They are working on a plan of their own to take over the shelter on the day of detonation. I am working with them."

"Can't you just kill the aliens and turn the bombs off?" Georgie asked.

"It's not that simple. They have been trying to figure out a way to disarm the satellites, but have had no luck yet, so we must make other plans just in case."

To be continued....

SEE MY FEATURED BOOKS AT
WWW.KIM-ROBINSON.COM

THE ROUX IN THE GUMBO

STREET LIFE TO HOUSE WIFE

STREET LIFE TO HOUSE WIFE 2

A CIVIL RIGHT TO LOVE

FOOD FOR THE SOUL

SWEEYT SATISFACTION

ABOUT THE AUTHOR

Kim Robinson is a wife and mother of three, residing in Dallas. She is also a seamstress and sewing instructor. You will find her on www. SewingSouls.com.

Her first novel came out in 2005 and achieved the Dallas Bestsellers list, as did her following works.

Literary Awards:

Capa Award
Disilgold Award
Literary World Award
And several others

When she is not writing, she is reading or watching movies. She is taking scriptwriting courses hoping to one day bring her work to the screen.

In October 2024, Kim received the Lifetime Achievement Award from President Biden for over thirty years of contributions. She is   a motivational speaker and the National spokesperson for Anna's House and Awayoutproject.org.

These organizations help survivors of Domestic Abuse and are instrumental in helping women start their lives anew.